The thought of leaving Ava behind left a hollowness in Colt's chest.

He cared about her, clearly. They needed each other right now and it was probably hard to think about leaving when he'd just gotten here, when they were at the start of their deal.

With Ryder in a carrier strapped to his chest, they went up and down the rows of the tree farm. "Jingle Bells" was playing on a speaker.

"That's the one," she said. "Not too big, not too small. Just right. It's a beauty."

It was. The tree was a Fraser fir, a good choice with its stiff branches that would hold lots of ornaments.

"It smells heavenly. Like Christmas." She laughed, and it felt good to see her happy, not worried or strained as she'd been in the car about finances. Or...unsure, like back at the house, when they'd been all over each other.

"What do you think, Ryder?" he asked. "A beaut, am I right?"

Ryder tried to bat at the branches, which told them he agreed.

"This is going to be a great Christmas, Ava," Colt said. He knew this because he was going to make sure of it.

Dear Reader,

As a single father of a four-month-old baby boy, Colt Dawson is still learning to distinguish between cries, figuring out his son's schedule and trying to be the father his baby deserves. But when he finds an unfinished letter stating that baby Ryder *isn't* his child, Colt's life turns upside down. He knows exactly who to go to for answers—Ava Guthrie. But will she tell him what he needs to know?

When Colt unexpectedly arrives at the failing alpaca ranch Ava inherited, he makes her a deal: *tell me the truth and I'll help turn your ranch around by Christmas*. Suddenly, two people out of their depth find more than they ever bargained for in each other— and in the holiday season.

I hope you enjoy Colt and Ava's story. Feel free to write me with any comments or questions at MelissaSenate@yahoo.com and visit my website, melissasenate.com, for more info about me and my books. For lots of photos of my cat and dog, friend me over on Facebook, Facebook.com/melissasenate.

Happy holidays and happy reading!

Melissa Senate

His Baby
No Matter What

———

MELISSA SENATE

HARLEQUIN
SPECIAL
EDITION

Recycling programs
for this product may
not exist in your area.

ISBN-13: 978-1-335-40818-1

His Baby No Matter What

Copyright © 2021 by Melissa Senate

Harlequin Enterprises ULC
22 Adelaide St. West, 40th Floor
Toronto, Ontario M5H 4E3, Canada
www.Harlequin.com

Printed in U.S.A.

Melissa Senate has written many novels for Harlequin and other publishers, including her debut, *See Jane Date*, which was made into a TV movie. She also wrote seven books for Harlequin Special Edition under the pen name Meg Maxwell. Her novels have been published in over twenty-five countries. Melissa lives on the coast of Maine with her teenage son; their rescue shepherd mix, Flash; and a lap cat named Cleo. For more information, please visit her website, melissasenate.com.

Chapter One

Four-month-old Ryder let out a short, shrill cry.

Colt Dawson bolted up from his chair and went over to the bassinet by the window, studying the baby who'd been fast asleep just a minute ago. Ryder's blue eyes were half-open. The eyes fluttered closed again, then sleepily lifted.

Colt ran down the possibilities. He'd been reading the book *Decoding Your Infant: A Primer for New Parents* and apparently there were more than fifteen different cries that meant different things. Short, shrill, he thought, trying to remember what that signified as he watched Ryder's eyes drift closed again, then lift a quarter way.

Let's see: his diaper needs changing. He's hungry. He has to burp. He has gas. He wants to be picked up. He's bored. He's still tired.

He wants his mother.

At that last one, Colt's heart felt so heavy he was surprised he didn't slump over.

Life could change in an instant, he'd always known. And it had.

Colt looked down at his son, eyes closed now, bow lips giving an Elvis Presley quirk, little chest covered in his World's Greatest Nephew pajamas— a gift from his aunt Haley—rising up and down. Ryder was fast asleep again.

He's fine, Colt told himself as he sat back down at his late wife's desk. Not every cry meant something, he recalled reading. *Give your baby a minute to self-soothe before you rush in to save the day. You'll teach valuable skills.* Next time, Colt vowed. He'd get this right eventually.

Ryder was probably dreaming of the floppy stuffed monkey Haley had brought over yesterday and the cry was in happy anticipation of shaking it again like a rattle. Or the bottle he knew would be coming when he woke up from his morning nap.

He's fine. You're fine. Everything is going to be fine.

Repeat.

One month had passed since they'd lost Ryder's mother to a car wreck. A month of shock and disorientation, a very sad funeral, of family over day and night, someone always leaping up from the sofa or guest room at 3:00 a.m. to check on Ryder when he cried—the long cries—so that Colt could get some rest, not that he could sleep a wink.

The Dawsons had filled his pantry, refrigerator and freezer to overflowing with meals with easy-to-follow reheating directions. There was always a pot of coffee going. A carton of eggnog in the fridge because his sister knew he loved it and Christmastime meant the grocery store had it in stock. Ryder's tiny clothes and burp cloths and blankies and binkies were always washed and put away neatly. Cleaning, from dusting to vacuuming to the dishwasher filled and emptied, happened like magic.

His sister and cousins and their spouses were the best people on earth.

Not that it was so different when Jocelyn had been alive. She'd taken care of everything. Colt was co-CEO of the company his grandfather had started with a partner fifty years ago. Godfrey and Dawson, run by Godfreys and Dawsons through this third generation, bought and sold companies across the West. Colt was often on the road or a plane and home only a couple of days a week, which had suited Jocelyn just fine.

And him, he thought, his collar squeezing his neck. A two-day-a-week dad. A *put the phone to his ear so I can tell him good night* dad. A milestone-missing dad. He shook his head.

He hadn't felt ready to be a father, not when he'd first gotten married at age twenty-four and not last year at thirty-three when Jocelyn had calmly said she was sick of his excuses and waiting for him to be ready and if he ever wanted sex again, they would *not* be using birth control. She'd cried, she'd pleaded, she'd reminded him that he'd said he would *probably* be ready to start a family when he was *thirty.* And so Colt had put aside his worries and given in to his wife's most fervent want. A baby. But month after month, she'd been disappointed. A year of trying. Their sex life becoming about fertile days. And Jocelyn's tears.

But their marriage had been in trouble for a few years by then, and when Jocelyn finally did get pregnant, nothing between them changed. The love, the tenderness, the sharing—all of it had slowly gone. He'd never forget the happiness on her face when she'd shown him the home pregnancy test stick with its bright pink plus sign. But the baby hadn't brought them closer.

Whether he'd been ready for fatherhood or not, though, at the sight of that plus sign, a surge of love and protectiveness had overtaken him, and with each passing day, he'd vowed to be the dad his child deserved. A great dad. His own father had been a serious workaholic like Colt was now. His parents had had a very traditional marriage and that was what Jocelyn had wanted, as well.

He hated—hated to the core of his being—that he'd actually re-created the home life he'd used to wish was different as a kid, as a teenager. That he *hadn't* talked to Jocelyn about.

For better or worse, for better or worse, for better or worse.

Another short, shrill cry came from the bassinet. Colt stood, but then reminded himself to give the baby a moment. He waited.

Silence. He'd gotten that one right.

He sat back down at the desk, his gaze on the hot pink nameplate engraved in gold cursive—*Jocelyn Dawson, Domestic Goddess*. He wasn't sure what to do with it. He'd put off sorting through her office and desk, but it was time. His sister and cousin Daisy had gone through her closet and donated most of it, packing away items that they thought Ryder might like to have one day, such as her favorite long cardigan that smelled of her perfume. He'd add the nameplate to that box.

His sister thought Jocelyn would have liked him to turn this room, her office on the first floor, into a playroom for Ryder, and that seemed like a good idea, but Colt had moved like molasses about going through her desk, the only thing left to do. He knew why, too.

Because deep down, he didn't want to live in this house—a stately white Colonial with a red door and black shutters, state-of-the-art everything, furnished down to the art on the walls by an interior decorator. The house, which had always reminded him of the one he'd grown up in, had never felt like home, not in all ten years they'd been here. But how could he sell Ryder's legacy— the house he'd lived in with his mother, albeit for just three short months—out from under him?

Which reminded him of a kind and tempting offer he'd gotten from his cousin Ford, a police detective here in Bear Ridge, the day after the funeral. Ford, a new dad himself with a six-month-old son, had stopped by with a giraffe rattle for Ryder and had found Colt in the nursery, putting Ryder's diaper on *backward*. That was when Ford had made the offer.

Come stay at one of the cabins at the ranch, his cousin had said. *You and Ryder. There's one miles out from the dude ranch, nothing but land and sky and mountain around it. Take a leave of absence from that job you hate. Let your son's*

*needs guide you and you'll be a pro at father-
hood at your own pace. Just let yourself be. Stay
as long as you want.*

Colt had felt like hell for how little he knew
about taking care of his own child. A helpless
baby. He couldn't even put on a diaper correctly?
Colt had been a traveling workaholic for years
and right back at it just a week after Ryder had
been born. Right back at it again until a month
ago when his entire world changed. But when
Ford had given him that chance to take a step
back, to spend more time with Ryder, to get out
of this house, he'd said not now, maybe later, time
isn't right, but thanks. Ford, to his credit and great
patience, hadn't said a word other than *Just give
it some thought.*

Colt had opened up to Ford more than he'd expected over the past year. He'd never been one to
share much about his personal life. Or what kept
him up at night. But over the months, he'd told
Ford a bit about his marriage and how rocky it
was. How he hadn't been ready to be a dad but
loved Ryder so much he sometimes thought his
heart would burst. How much he did hate his job
and how he'd ended up there in the first place.
The weight—the crushing weight of it.

And he'd talked a lot about what he'd once

wanted to do with his life. His dream had always been to be a cowboy. A rancher with a good-sized spread, cattle and sheep, a few horses and, of course, a dog, the border collie he'd always longed for as a kid. Black and white and running around smiling the way border collies did.

So yes, he'd thought hard about Ford's offer.

But his responsibilities at Godfrey and Dawson were so far-reaching, affected so many people, that he couldn't just take a month off to spend in the wilderness. Even a week off. His co-CEO had been recuperating from a bad case of the flu and there were mergers and acquisitions up in the air that Colt and his team needed to deal with and deal with well. So he'd gone back to work, full speed.

Godfrey and Dawson are counting on you? his sister had repeated when he told her about Ford's offer and why he'd turned it down. *Come on, Colt. That's just years of pressure from Dad talking. I'll tell you who's counting on you:* your son.

Knife to the heart.

Of course Haley was right.

But then he'd hear his widowed father's deathbed questions, barely managed with the last of his voice during those final heartbreaking days in hospice. Colt had been just twenty-one years old, about to graduate with a business degree from the university Bertrand Dawson had insisted on, demanding Colt forget about this "ranch nonsense." Colt had figured that if he was going to be a rancher—and hell yes, he was going to defy his father and follow his own path—and run his own cattle operation, he'd need those educational tools, so he'd agreed to business school. Which had his father holding his tongue about Colt's insistence on spending his summers as a cowboy, where he learned the ranching business from the ground up. He'd never been so happy as when he'd been herding cattle or sheep on a mare, fixing broken fence in the pouring rain, mucking out stalls and grooming the horses. Once he graduated from college, he'd been planning on telling his dad that he was going to take an assistant foreman job at the prosperous Wild K Ranch a town over.

According to Bertrand Dawson, Colt was born to become CEO of Godfrey and Dawson, just as Bertrand had been. The way Colt saw it, he was born to work the land.

But then his father's heart started failing.

Colt, I can go at peace if I know you're going to take over as the bright and shining new Dawson of Godfrey and Dawson, just like I took over from my father, his dad had said from his hospice bed, both frail hands holding on to Colt's. *It's your history. Your legacy. One day, your son will be the Dawson of Godfrey and Dawson...*

That last part twisted his gut. There was no point arguing with a dying man that if Colt did ever have a child, boy or girl, that child would follow their heart. Besides, Colt wasn't planning on having children. And that he'd never brought up with his father. An heir was expected. Period. But at twenty-one, Colt figured anything was possible, that maybe he'd change his mind.

You'll take over for me at Godfrey and Dawson? his dad had asked just hours before he passed, uncharacteristic tears in his blue eyes. There had been desperate hope, the culmination of all his father's dreams, in that question. His sister, a few months shy of eighteen, stood shaking by the window, tears pouring down her face.

What else could Colt have said but *Yes, Dad. Of course I will.*

And mean it, accept it, become the bright shining new Dawson at Godfrey and Dawson.

I always knew I could count on you, Colt, Bertrand had said, a peace on his face, pride in his whisper.

And that had been that. Thirteen years ago, he'd made a promise to his dying father. He'd needed to take care of Haley, just a senior in high school then. He'd turned down the assistant foreman job. He'd shadowed his father's counterpart, a good, honest man—whose own son was now Colt's counterpart—at Godfrey and Dawson during twelve-hour days until he knew the business. He'd worked his way up to co-CEO within a few years, living and breathing the role.

He'd hung up his cowboy hat for his dad's expensive leather briefcase, which he used every day as a reminder of his promise.

So yes, he'd thought hard about Ford's offer. A month at the Dawson Family Guest Ranch, a sprawling popular dude ranch a half hour outside town. He loved that place. He'd taken Jocelyn there once and stayed in their "luxe" cabin, but she'd hated everything about it. The dust. The bugs. The smell of the horses. There was something in that memory, combined with her sudden, shocking loss, and hearing his father's hopeful questions banging around his head. When Jocelyn died, he'd taken two days of bereavement leave and then gone back to work.

But while he'd been at Godfrey and Dawson this past month, Ryder *was* at the ranch. The place had a great day care managed by his cousin-in-law Maisey and there were many little Dawsons crawling and running around their huge space in the lodge. Every night, when he'd arrived to pick up Ryder, he'd breathe in all that wilderness and for just that moment, he'd feel a peace he hadn't experienced since his days as a cowboy.

Then every night this past month, he'd bring Ryder back to the big house in town, trying to adhere to the schedule Jocelyn had kept magnetized to the fridge, trying to change Ryder's diaper without getting sprayed or putting the diaper on backward—that had happened two more times until he figured it out—how to get through bath time without soaking the floor in water and BabyClean shampoo, which smelled heavenly. The schedule helped since he knew when to give Ryder his bottle, and his cousins had reminded him to pat him on the back to get him to burp. When they saw how he fumbled, the strain on his face, they took over—to Colt's relief.

He'd had a month of nights and weekends with his son, which, granted, wasn't exactly a lot, but he'd hoped he'd get better at the basics of baby care and he hadn't. Fatherhood just didn't come naturally to him. Maybe because of how he'd grown up—with a father in the distance. And maybe because Jocelyn had wanted them in their traditional roles and always said no to his offers to help. Or maybe Colt just wasn't comfortable.

All the above.

But now, the only thing that mattered was that he had a baby to raise—right and well—and he was trying. Every day. Thank God he had his sister and cousins. Colt and Haley had only a small extended family scattered across the West. Jocelyn had been raised in foster care, so Ryder didn't have any family on his mother's side. Between Haley and the Dawson cousins, Ryder would grow up with a big, loud, loving clan, and that gave Colt no small measure of relief.

Thing was, Colt was now a single father. Working seventy hours a week, traveling, being away from Ryder when his mother was gone made Colt feel like hell, like he was doing something wrong. Very wrong.

And since thinking about it tore at his gut, whenever he did let it creep into his mind, he'd make himself busy with necessary chores. Like right now. While his son slept, Colt should be sorting through Jocelyn's desk, making file or shred piles.

He glanced over at the bassinet. Not a peep. *Get it done, Colt*, he ordered himself.

Colt opened the top drawer of the desk. Mostly

supplies—pens, pencils, paper clips, Post-its—the usual stuff. He dropped everything in a box, which he planned to donate to the local schools. He tried to open the side drawer but it was locked or jammed. He looked in the box to make sure he hadn't dropped a key in without realizing it, then found it by accident when the top of his leg scraped against the underside of the desk. The key was taped there.

Interesting. A well-hidden key usually meant something to hide. Maybe he'd find Jocelyn's diaries, not that he'd invade her privacy or even want to know more than he already did. He slid in the key and turned. Inside was only her stationery, a long narrow pad with her name in cursive at the top, and matching envelopes. The start of a letter to Ava—her best friend—was on the top page in Jocelyn's unmistakable handwriting. The letter was unfinished and stopped midsentence as if Jocelyn had either gotten interrupted or changed her mind about writing.

Dear Ava,
After all we've been through and shared, I can't believe you won't give me the assurance I need that you'll never tell Colt the truth. Have I ever asked you for anything

*other than your friendship before? No. Now
I'm asking for something very important to
me and you can't do it? Screw you. Colt
will never find out that Ryder isn't his child.
If you can't promise never to tell him, our
friendship is over. I wish you'd*

Colt froze, the letter fluttering out of his hands
into the open drawer. What. The. Hell.

He snatched it back and reread it. *Colt will
never*—"never" underlined—*find out that Ryder
isn't his child...*

He shook his head, shock and confusion over-
whelming him, his brain warring against what
was in black and white in his wife's handwriting.

Ryder wasn't his son?

What?

Jocelyn had had an affair?

The doorbell rang and he ignored it. He didn't
want to see anyone, couldn't see anyone right
now.

A second later, his phone pinged with a text.
His sister, Haley.

You home? Your car's here. I'm on the porch. I
have something adorable for Ryder but it might
be too big.

Okay. Haley, he could see. Haley, he could talk to. He ran to the door and the moment he opened it, his sister rushed past him, a bag dangling off each wrist.

"I've got today's special from the diner and a really cute fleece winter suit with bear ears for Ryder," she said in a rush of words, Haley-style, heading for the kitchen, her long golden braid swishing behind her. "I think the saleswoman said it was called a bunting? Oh, this is shepherd's pie," she added, lifting her left wrist with the bag from the Bear Ridge Diner, where she worked as a waitress. "And there's a slice of chocolate layer cake in there, too."

He slowly followed her into the kitchen on autopilot, watching her put the containers in the fridge.

"Low on eggnog," she said, giving the container a shake. "I don't know how you can drink that thick, slimy stuff." She put it back in the fridge, taking out her phone and no doubt typing a note to pick up more eggnog for her older brother, whom everyone was doing *way* too much for at this point. "Oh, and I was thinking that we should go to Abbott's Christmas tree farm, Colt. You still don't have a tree up and, yeah, I get it, this isn't exactly a festive time, but a trimmed tree will cheer this place up and it's for Ryder, really."

Haley was a talker. He loved his sister to pieces and right now, he was grateful that she was going a mile a minute, reaching into the other bag to pull out a tan-colored fleece snowsuit with bear ears, because he couldn't form words yet. He could barely breathe.

"Think it's too big?" she asked, holding it up. "It's size six to twelve months." She peered at him. "Colt?"

Nothing would come out of his mouth. He stood there, unable to speak.

She was staring at him now. "Colt? What's wrong?"

He closed his eyes for a second and then left the room, Haley hot on his heels.

"Jesus, Colt, you're scaring me to death. What's going on? Is Ryder sick?"

He went into Jocelyn's office. If he looked toward the bassinet, he'd fall apart. So instead he just handed Haley the stationery pad, the unfinished letter in black ink.

Her eyes widened as she read. She looked up at him. "What. The. Hell?"

"That's what I said. I just found it. A minute before you rang the bell. I was going through her desk to clear it. The drawer was locked and I found this. Ryder isn't mine?"

"We don't know that *for sure*," she said, eying the letter with a wince, then dropping the pad—facedown on the desk. "We don't know anything for sure. It's unfinished, and we don't know when she wrote this or if she was sure herself or what."

"She sounds very sure in the letter," he said. Chills ran up and down his spine.

Ryder let out another little cry and Colt instinctively rushed over. The baby's eyes were still closed, his little hand now raised by his head, which was covered in an orange-and-white cotton cap. He stared down at the baby he loved so much.

"He's not my son?" *That can't be true.*

"He is your son, Colt. Nothing changes that."

But life wasn't the same as it was five minutes ago. And nothing would change *that*.

He sucked in a breath and paced by the window.

"What are you thinking?" Haley asked gently.

He was thinking about Ava Guthrie, Jocelyn's best friend, to whom she'd been writing the letter. Very soon after Ryder was born, Ava had inherited a ranch a couple of hours away, a falling-down mess, Jocelyn had called it, which was why she hadn't been around.

She'd come to Jocelyn's funeral, though. He hadn't noticed her until she'd suddenly appeared in the receiving line, her blond hair a stark contrast against her black dress, a small hat with a short black veil shielding her face, her eyes. She'd offered quick condolences, which surprised him, given how close she and Jocelyn had been. He'd been holding Ryder in his arms, and she'd touched the baby's cheek, and then she was gone.

"I'm going to see Ava for answers," he said. "Right now."

Chapter Two

Ava Guthrie parked the wheelbarrow full of straw inside the barn and grabbed a heap to make fresh bedding for the alpacas. Princess, living up to her name, liked extra padding in her sleep nook. Lorelai and Rory, mother and daughter and both the same snowy white, always huddled together, so they required straw spread out in their section of the large pen by the window. Pecan and Cookie, senior citizens who were both eighteen years old, expected nightly treasures buried in their straw, like two small bites of carrot for each. And the smallest of the six gals, Star with her tricolored fleece, was a bit of a loner and never asked for much.

Ava glanced out the arched window to see the six sweet alpacas grazing in the near pasture, the snow just starting to fall. A storm was coming late this afternoon and soon the fields would be covered, but Ava was prepared for winter. Four months ago, when she'd inherited this ranch, she'd been scared to death. She hadn't known an alpaca from a donkey. Now, she knew what she was doing enough to get by, enough to keep the six not just alive but well.

She owed that much to her great-aunt Iris. The fiercely independent never-married seventy-year-old had run the ranch herself, but apparently she'd chalked her aches and dizziness to aging and hard work instead of illness until it had been too late. Ava hadn't known Iris at all—she'd estranged herself from her small family when Ava was just a little kid—but had always wanted to learn her story and secrets.

The sound of a vehicle coming up the long dirt driveway caught her attention, and she headed out of the barn to see who it might be. Iris's funeral had been sparse, just a few fellow ranchers and two women, one in her late forties and the other in her sixties, who'd been the members of Iris's knitting circle and used the alpacas' fine-spun fleece as yarn. They'd asked if Ava was going to start holding the knitting group every Monday and Thursday as Iris had, and Ava had felt bad having to say no, that she'd never learned how to knit and would be up to her ears just catching up on basic ranching skills. The women had nodded and every so often, one of them would stop by to say hello and drop off a cake or pie, which she appreciated, but Ava rarely had time to sit down and talk. Last time it had been Maria who'd come, so it was likely Vivi now.

But once again, Ava wasn't up for company. She'd determined that today would be the day she'd make a plan of action. For getting the ranch back to where it had been before Iris had taken ill.

Until now, Ava had been reacting instead of acting. Taking care of business, running herself ragged with the chores and upkeep. Because of grief, she knew. She'd lost her fiancé when he broke up with her just days before their wedding for reasons that made her chest ache. She'd lost the aunt she'd always wanted to get to know. She'd lost her best friend and then any chance to see Jocelyn's baby grow up.

After her guest left she'd sit down with coffee and her laptop and make lists. Including how to get the ranch ready for a Christmas festival when Christmas was only three weeks away. The festival would let the area folks know the Prairie Hills Alpaca Ranch was open for visitors. Iris used to offer all kinds of programs, from day tours to summer camps and after-school classes where kids got to be junior alpaca farmers, to knitting workshops, and Ava wanted to reinstate all that come spring. If she could learn to run an alpaca ranch, she could teach a basic farm unit and learn to knit enough to teach a beginner class. She hoped, anyway.

An expensive black SUV came into view. Vivi drove a small red car so it wasn't her. As the SUV got closer, Ava could see it was a man driving. She left the barn and walked over to the porch steps, waiting. Who could this be?

As the car got closer and pulled up in front of the house, her stomach dropped.

Oh God. Was that Jocelyn's husband?

The man wore dark sunglasses so she couldn't quite tell, but there was always something unmistakable about Colt Dawson, his good looks and strong presence filling a room or a wide-open space. She squinted, shielding her eyes from the bright winter sun as she tried to see.

Yes, that was Colt getting out of the vehicle and taking off the sunglasses, which he put in his pocket. He wore a brown leather barn coat, jeans, work boots, his short brown hair under a Stetson. Had she ever seen him look like that? Like a cowboy. He turned her way for a moment, then held up a hand as a greeting before moving to the back passenger door. He walked toward her carrying Ryder in his car seat.

Her gaze fixed on the baby. Ryder. How she'd missed him. He'd been a tiny newborn, just a week old, the last time she'd seen him—well, except for the funeral a month ago but she'd left immediately after the service. She'd offered her condolences to Colt and he'd looked at her with such compassion. He'd lost his wife, she'd lost her best friend, but of course he wouldn't have known that she and Jocelyn had stopped speaking a week after Ryder was born.

What would bring Colt—

She gasped, hand flying to her mouth when she suddenly realized exactly what would bring Colt all the way out here. Without warning. Without word. Not a call or a text.

He *knew*.

Ava sucked in a breath, wondering how this conversation was going to go. He stopped a few feet away from her, and she could see Colt was equal parts conflicted, angry, full of questions.

Yes. He knew.

"Ava," he said with a nod.

"It's nice to see you again." She instantly wished she could take back such a trite line. She bent down to the baby, her heart constricting. Beautiful, sweet Ryder. There were traces of Jocelyn in his expression, in the shape of his blue eyes. "He's gotten so big."

She bit her lip, waiting for what she knew was coming.

He cleared his throat. "I was cleaning out Jocelyn's desk and found a letter she'd started to you. Apparently, Ryder's not my child."

Oh God. She'd wondered a few times if he'd find out and how.

"Who's his father, Ava?" The ice in his voice sent chills up her spine.

He was staring at her so hard that she glanced past him at the alpacas, but a babbling sound from Ryder brought her attention back. Colt, too, was now focused on Ryder.

She'd often wondered what the past month was like for him, alone with a baby when he wasn't used to being home at all. She'd thought a lot about Colt Dawson, actually—ever since Jocelyn had blurted out the truth to her. That Colt wasn't his father.

Promise me you'll never tell…

Ava zipped up her down jacket to the top as a gust of wind whipped her hair, the snow starting to fall in earnest now. "It's cold. Let's go inside."

She knew he wanted her to just spit out the

name, not that she could, of course, but he clearly also knew this would require a sit-down conversation, so he nodded.

She led the way up the three green wood stairs, rickety in one spot and peeling everywhere. The storm door was barely hanging on. She never really paid attention to how run-down the place was until someone came by, then she saw it through their eyes.

But, of course, Colt wasn't there to say hi or see the ranch she'd inherited.

Once inside, Ava shut the door against the cold. Colt set the carrier on the round rug and knelt in front of it, unbuckling the harness and lifting Ryder out.

"Can I hold him?" she asked.

"If it gets me the truth, sure," he said.

She glanced up at Colt, his blue eyes intense and so focused on her that she had to look away again. She held out her arms. Ryder came to her easily, and the breath almost went out of her. That final argument with Jocelyn still had its grip on her heart and squeezed now. She shut her eyes against it and concentrated on Ryder, the pure, small joy of seeing him again, of holding him. A piece of her best friend. No matter how things had ended.

"Well, I asked you a direct question and you're not answering, so I guess holding Ryder isn't enough," he said, practically snatching the baby from her arms. "I'll make you a deal, Ava."

She whirled to face him. Colt Dawson was first and foremost a businessman. "What deal? We don't need a deal."

He glanced around, then walked over to the window overlooking the side of the porch and the fields, a dusting of snow already on the ground. "You've been here four months and the place is falling down around you." He looked out, then turned back to face her. "I saw the condition of some of the fencing as I drove up. The porch steps. The house. The barn doors. Today's going to be the first real snowfall. You don't want to mess with Wyoming wind chill and blizzards without sturdy structures. You tell me what I need to know and I'll help you out around here today before the snow gets bad. I spent summers all through high school and college working on ranches."

Oh, Colt. "You don't have to do anything to get the truth out of me. I always thought you deserved to know."

He froze. "So it's definitely true," he said, and the look on his face fractured her heart. Anguish. "I'm not his father."

She shook her head. "I'm so sorry, Colt."

He held Ryder more closely against him, a hand protectively on his back. He tilted his head down and rested it very gently on the baby's head.

He was Ryder's father in every way that mattered. He had to know that.

"I need…a minute," he said, not looking at her. Not looking at Ryder.

She nodded and hurried upstairs, wishing she could stay with him, wishing she had the right words.

She went into her bedroom and closed the door, her heart beating so fast she could hear it in her ears, forcing herself to give him the privacy he deserved. As she stood there, in shock herself, she realized just how little she knew Colt Dawson or how he felt right now.

Maybe he'd never look at Ryder the same way again.

Colt walked back over to the windows with the view of the alpacas, trying not to hold Ryder too tightly. As if keeping him close would make this all go away.

Not mine, not mine, not mine…

He dropped down into a club chair by the window, his air practically gone, his legs like rubber, his head full of static.

Before the letter, Ryder had been his beloved son, his child, his future. *And now?* he thought, bitterness snaking its way into his stomach and up to his throat. *Just like that, he's not?*

I waited for you for the seven months I knew you were coming, Ryder. I was there when you were born. I've rushed up to the nursery after work and business trips just to watch you breathe. I've stared at you for hours on end, in total wonder that you exist, that I could feel this way about anyone—this love, so pure and big. I've tried to take care of you this past month now that it's just the two of us.

But you're not my child?

Like hell, he wasn't. Colt gently leaned his head down against the baby's again. Ryder was as much his child as he was before he found that damned key and the letter.

"You're my baby no matter what," he whispered into the soft brown hair. "You hear me? You're my son. Love makes it so. My name on your birth certificate makes it so."

There was no *question*, no doubt of how Colt felt about Ryder Dawson, bombshell be damned. So if all that was a given, why did he feel like his heart was run over by an eighteen-wheeler? His chest physically ached.

He reached into his pocket and texted Haley with his left hand, a feat in itself.

It's true. But like you said, like I just said to myself, he's my son no matter what. So why do I feel so damned bad?

She responded right away: Because of the lie. The betrayal. That'll sting less with the days and weeks ahead. Just take some time to yourself, Colt. Take Ford up on his offer and just be in the wilderness with Ryder at the dude ranch through Christmas. I'm seriously begging you not to go back to Godless and Dawdling till the new year. Let yourself have some time to just be.

How the Godless and Dawdling got a smile out of him he had no idea. I'm still at Ava's alpaca ranch. There's more to talk about so we'll see. I'll call you soon.

Love you and love my nephew, she texted back, adding an emotion of a smiley face wearing a cowboy hat.

He stood up again and took Ryder over to the window. One of the alpacas, a big white one, seemed to be staring right at Colt. Funny-looking creature.

"You see that thing?" Colt asked Ryder, shifting the baby in his arms. "That's an alpaca. I've seen them before but I don't know much about them. Did I hear they don't have teeth? That can't be right. We can ask Ava later."

Ryder waved his hand almost like he was waving hello to the long-necked furry animal with a clump of hair/fur on its head who was now standing extremely close to another white alpaca.

Colt was talking to Ryder like he always did. As if he hadn't just had his world turned upside down. Because the news didn't change anything, he figured. It just…sat on his chest like a baby elephant.

"Godless and Dawdling," he whispered, shaking his head. His sister had a lot of names for the corporation that she felt their dad had chosen over them, over their mother, over birthday parties and help with math. "I don't have a fact in my head, Ryder. Not a sales figure. Not a projection. Not an analysis of Wilkin Industries, which we're buying this week. All gone from my head. Nothing in here," he said, giving the left side of his skull a knock. "So yeah, don't think I'm making it into the office tomorrow." *Or Tuesday*, he thought, looking at the snow coming down.

And when Ava finally would tell him who Ryder's biological father was, he'd probably need another week to deal with that. He'd stew in his corner office, trying to distract himself from the sickening truth with work. Who was it? Whose DNA, whose blood coursed through his son's body?

Their accountant. Their lawyer. That old boyfriend from Jocelyn's tenth high school reunion. Her tennis coach.

Or some man she seduced in a bar specifically to get herself pregnant.

Maybe an affair. A long-term lie of a romance that had been going on for who knew how long. Right under his damned nose.

It was one of those.

He closed his eyes, the ache in his chest getting worse, tighter.

The lie. The betrayal. His sister was absolutely right. Colt was a lot of things, but he didn't lie, he didn't cheat, he didn't steal. He believed in ethics, responsibility. He'd caught Jocelyn in silly white lies over the years and had always told her she didn't have to make stuff up, that he'd always rather know the truth about something, no matter how minor, than be blissfully ignorant. An oxymoron, in his opinion. She would cancel a dinner date with his co-CEO and his wife because of a headache when Jocelyn was feeling fine and just couldn't stand the wife. Just tell him *that*.

Maybe the truth would have brought them closer instead of Colt handing her two aspirin she didn't need and giving her space to rest when they could have been talking about how Godfrey's wife was on the snooty side. At a fundraiser, a woman had asked Jocelyn where she'd grown up, and she'd said: *My parents have a gorgeous Queen Anne Victorian close to town with a pool and a skating rink in the back fields. What a lovely place to grow up.*

Her parents had died when she was four and they'd lived in a cramped apartment above a bar then. He'd chalked up her response to how bad she felt about her past, and really, what was a white lie, a fantasy she'd wished were true, to someone who didn't give Jocelyn a second thought?

He should have paid more attention to her casually tossed lies.

Colt shifted Ryder in his arms, breathing in the baby-soap scent of him. He stayed in front of the window, staring past the alpacas at the snow-dusted land, the fencing, the evergreens in the distance, the mountain range. "A person can think in a place like this," he whispered to Ryder.

But what was he thinking right then was about the biological father. Who. What. Where. When.

Did he even want to know who the father was? *He* was the father. That was all that mattered.

Being a father was all that mattered. And Colt would give himself the kind of performance review that would not only result in no end-of-the-year bonus, but that would put him on probation.

I could have lost you, too, he thought, holding Ryder a bit closer. *The accident could have happened on any slickened road before your mother dropped you off at the day care for the morning.*

I could have lost you.

He had to change. He had to put Ryder first. Not Godless and Dawdling. His father might have seen it differently—how to raise a family, what the priorities were. Colt wasn't Bertrand Dawson.

But how could he take Haley's advice, Ford's advice, and actually let himself have this time with Ryder through Christmas? He needed to be at work on Wednesday. There was a lot going on, complicated deals, so many balls in the air, moving parts, and yes, he had good people working for him, but he needed to be there, involved in the steps to ensure everything ran smoothly, that fires were put out and well.

Not that I don't need time on a ranch, he

thought, watching the alpacas, one of them doing her own thing at the other end of the pasture. The small one, tricolored.

"There's the lone wolf," he said to Ryder, nodding at the furry black, brown and tan creature. "The one who blazes her own path, doesn't follow the herd. That used to be me, once upon a time."

Every now and then he'd notice his old cowboy hat, the one from his last job on the Wild K the summer before he graduated from college, on the top shelf of his closet. He hadn't put that on his head in almost fifteen years—until today, until he knew he was driving out to a ranch. He'd laced up his old scuffed work boots, too. The softened-up brown leather ones that were more comfortable than any of the Italian-maker shoes he owned.

I don't know anything right now, Ryder. I just know you're my son, end of story. End of letter.

With that, the ache in his chest, the tightness lifted a bit, he headed up the stairs with Ryder, no idea where he was going. At the top of the landing, the hallway walls a strange dark pink, he stopped.

"Ava?" he called out.

He heard a door open and there she was, her hazel eyes holding worry, her hands clasping and unclasping.

"I owe you an apology," he said. "I barged over here to your ranch, no call, nothing. I demanded information and then when I got it, I actually pretty much told you to leave so I could have the room to myself. I'm not CEO here. And this is *your* house."

The hands unclasped, the worry dissipating some. "I get it, Colt. No apologies."

She was kinder than he deserved. "I don't think I want to know who the father is. It doesn't matter. I'm the father."

She gasped. "Oh God. I should have said this right away. Jocelyn didn't cheat on you. There is no biological father. I mean, other than the science of it."

He tilted his head. "What?"

"She was artificially inseminated through a fertility clinic using a sperm bank," Ava explained.

The air whooshed out of him much like it had when he'd found that letter, but now the shock felt more like surprise. "A sperm bank," he repeated, the words slowly processing through his brain.

Ava nodded, glancing at Ryder, then back at Colt. "She wasn't getting pregnant the traditional way, as you know," she added with a wince. "So she…decided to, uh, take matters into her own hands."

Into her own hands. Those words repeated in his head.

"She said she chose a donor whose profile noted he had brown hair and blue eyes. Like you," Ava went on as if rushing to fill the silence from him. "Tall, like you. A college student getting a business degree, like you once were."

He closed his eyes for a second, the lie getting bigger, the betrayal even uglier. Chills ran up his spine, despite the fact that he was standing here in his heavy leather barn coat. The lengths Jocelyn had gone to make him think he was the father. Why? Their marriage hadn't been close to okay, let alone good. She could have left him, found love with someone else, started a family with someone else. Why go through the subterfuge, the deceit?

As if she knew what he was thinking, Ava said, "She did love you, Colt. And she liked her lifestyle, she liked her house, she liked that her husband was co-CEO of a half-century-old corporation. She liked that you traveled the West and always brought her back a piece of jewelry from whatever city or town you went."

Her lifestyle. "I feel sick to my stomach," he said.

"I don't know why I said all that." She shook her head. "I need to just stop talking."

"No," he said. "I want to understand. I'm glad you said all that."

The narrow shoulders, all bunched moments ago, relaxed. Ava was tall, five eight, five nine, but slight. There were faint shadows under her hazel eyes, her hair pulled back from a face completely free of makeup. She wore a long, thick off-white cardigan tied with a sash around her waist and black leggings and she had her arms wrapped around herself as if she were either cold or just very, very tired.

He'd guess tired. And he was adding to it, no doubt.

"Your name is on the birth certificate, Colt," she said, again her gaze dropping to Ryder before lifting back to him. "*You* are Ryder's father. That was very important to her, that *that* be irrefutable. She looked into all the legalities."

He nodded on a sigh. He couldn't talk about this anymore right now. Or he'd punch a wall. *Try changing a diaper with a broken hand*, he thought. *So just drop it right now.*

"I'm desperate for a cup of coffee or two," he said. "Lead the way to the kitchen and I'll make a pot."

"I've got it," she said, practically running past him down the stairs as if grateful for the escape, somewhere to go, something to do besides being trapped in this dark pink hallway by him, a big guy still in his coat and cowboy hat, holding a baby.

He'd probably spoken to Ava a total of twenty minutes in the ten years he'd known her. But she could likely write a book about him. She must know everything about him, everything about how his marriage had been, what kind of father he was.

He headed down after her, unsettled, the ache back in his chest.

Chapter Three

Ava stopped just before the kitchen doorway, her heart beating so fast she had to gulp in a breath.

That. Was. Intense.

"I'll take Ryder so you can get out of your coat," she said.

"Something I had to learn how to do over the past month." He scooched Ryder up in one arm while using the other hand to unzip his coat. He shrugged out of one side, then shifted the baby to his other arm and got the coat off, grabbing it before it could hit the floor. "I'm not great at fatherhood, but I can get out of my coat and not drop Ryder on his head."

She smiled, taking the coat from him, and then his hat. "You probably just never had much opportunity to show your chops. But the past month, you must have learned a lot about taking care of a baby."

"I wish I could say that's true. But I went back to work two days after and Ryder went to the excellent day care at my family's dude ranch. Plus my sister and cousins were always around, changing a diaper, making a bottle, doing the laundry. Nothing has really changed." He looked down as he said that last part, and she could see how his own words must have been bitter on his tongue. "Yeah, I'm some father. Outsourcing it all."

Oh, Colt, she thought. *Even I can see how much you love your son and I barely know you.* But *feelings* weren't going to be at the top of a corporate man's hierarchy. Actions were. Deliverables. All that company lingo. "Let me hang these up," she said, knowing he'd be glad for the change of subject, even for a minute. She hung both on the row of hooks by the front door. "Let's go have that coffee."

He nodded. "All of it."

She gave him a commiserating smile, unable to take her eyes off him for a moment. No, she definitely had never seen him look this way before. His tall—six feet two or three—muscular frame was in faded jeans, a long-sleeved dark-blue Henley shirt, brown leather work boots.

She headed into the big country kitchen and he followed, taking a seat at the white pedestal table. Ryder was content on his lap with his binkie, a cartoon orange tiger on the end.

Colt looked around the large square room. "That refrigerator must be fifty years old."

She nodded. "Probably. Works, though. That's how I judge things around here."

He nodded back. She felt his eyes on her a few times as she poured the water in the carafe and got out the mugs, carrying over a small round tray of cream and sugar.

"I brought the letter if you want to read it," he said.

She practically jumped, the tray thudding on the table.

"Sorry," he said. He shook his head. "Forget I said that. But I have it if you ever do want to see it. I guess I just wanted you to know that."

The scent of hazelnut coffee filled the air. She needed a cup bad.

"I probably will want to read it at some point," she said. "Not today. Probably not in a month, either. Everything about that letter, whatever it said, will be painful to me, Colt."

"I figure," he said gently. "It was unfinished and just a few lines, if that helps."

She glanced at him and sat down. "Actually, it does. Did she say I was no longer her best friend?" They'd been friends since high school, both of them a year younger than Colt at the huge regional high school, so they hadn't known him in those days. Jocelyn had big plans to move to Hollywood and become an actress, but she'd always worked at the Bear Ridge pizzeria, boyfriends keeping her rooted to town. When she'd met Colt at twenty-one, he was already a bigwig at his family corporation and she'd felt she'd found her star, her Prince Charming, in him. She'd never left Bear Ridge.

He stared at her for a moment, sudden compassion in his eyes. "No. She didn't say anything about that. She was definitely angry that you wouldn't promise not to tell me the truth. That much she made clear. You refused to promise and it caused a rift?"

She nodded, feeling so alone again. For months she'd fought that feeling by visiting the alpacas, talking to them, and they were such a funny-looking, sweet crew that they always cheered her up. She needed them as much as they needed her.

"I inherited this ranch just before Ryder was born," she said, getting up to pour the coffee. "I'd planned on making the two-hour drive a couple times a month to visit or she'd drive out with the baby. But Ryder was just a couple days old when she told me that you weren't his father. Just a week old when she said I wasn't welcome in your lives if I wouldn't make the promise never to tell you. We never spoke again. A month ago, you called me about the accident."

"I didn't know you and Jocelyn were on the outs. There's a lot I didn't know, apparently."

She looked at Ryder, his sweet little face, and Jocelyn's accusations started clanging around her head. Her chest clenched.

"You okay?" he asked.

She gave something of a shrug and brought over the two filled mugs, then sat back down across from Colt. "Not really. You?"

"Nope," he said. "Not okay at all." He reached his arm out and covered her hand for a moment, the thoughtfulness, the warmth of his big, strong hand so comforting. "You must hate me," he suddenly said, pulling back his hand and picking up his mug and leaning far over the table to drink it, careful, she noted, to keep it away from where little batting hands could get it.

"Hate you?" she repeated. "Why would I hate you?"

"You were my wife's best friend. I didn't exactly make her happy."

She shook her head. "She really did love you, Colt. She loved her life. She *didn't* love that you didn't want to start a family those first years you were married. She talked a lot about that. But once she got pregnant, she had everything she ever wanted. Jocelyn was a foster kid on a busy farm that she despised. She was lonely and never got adopted and aged out alone in Bear Ridge. She met you when she was behind the counter of a hot pizzeria dreaming of bigger things. You changed her entire world, Colt."

"But in the end, I didn't give her what she wanted. She had to make it happen for herself."

Ava stared at him, taking that in. She hadn't thought of it that way before. "Well, that was Jocelyn, wasn't it? Scrappy. She got you, didn't she? Most eligible bachelor in Bear Ridge, Wyoming."

Now he seemed to be taking *that* in, but she couldn't read his expression.

She had a feeling he was thinking that there was a big difference between scrappy, make-it-happen and *ugly deceit to get what you want*.

"I can't tell you how much it helps to talk to you, Ava. I know there's a lot going unsaid that we don't even have to broach."

Yes, that exactly. She nodded and could feel his eyes on her as she glanced down at her coffee, wrapping her hands around the hot mug.

For all she did know of Colt Dawson, she really didn't *know* him. She was just beginning to understand the depth of how little.

Ryder yawned suddenly, his eyes drooping.

"I'll go get his baby seat," Ava said, bolting up, not realizing until she did that she needed a minute to herself. A minute away from the intensity of Colt's blue eyes on her, the way he filled up the room. "Will he nap in it? If not, I actually have something of a nursery upstairs in the guest room. From before the falling-out. I thought she'd come with Ryder and the ranch would be like their own personal petting zoo."

"Didn't expect me to join, no doubt," he said.

"You traveled a lot. Do you still? I mean, this past month?"

He glanced out the window and sipped his coffee, and then nodded. "I have to make some changes."

She held his gaze for a second, then hurried out of the room, trying to catch her breath when she was out of the doorway.

What was it about him? His presence was so… outsized. It wasn't just that he was six three and had shoulders that practically stretched across the kitchen. There was something in his eyes, in his voice, in the way she could see his heart, all bruised and battered, which he blamed himself for, clearly. He was open and shut at the same time.

She picked up the carrier and brought it back. Colt settled the baby inside and buckled it, then set it on the far side of the table. For a moment they both watched Ryder fight his nap, eyes drooping, drooping and finally closing, then sleepily lifting before closing for good.

"He's so beautiful," she said. "Those cheeks, my God."

"I always thought he looked a lot like me," Colt said. "Because of the brown hair, the blue eyes. Otherwise he favors Jocelyn…"

She looked at beautiful Ryder, that gorgeous face, the big cheeks. Earlier she'd been worried that Colt would think different of Ryder now that he knew the truth. But she hadn't factored in that he'd literally look differently at him. The baby he always assumed was a mini-him wasn't. Not in the slightest. Just the right hair color. The right eye color.

Again she felt that chill run along the nape of her neck at the subterfuge. She knew what Jocelyn would say if she were sitting right here, the one sipping coffee with her instead of the husband she'd left behind.

I got what I wanted and it turns out he enjoys

fatherhood and loves Ryder to pieces, so where's the harm? Everything worked out fine.

Ava let out an inward sigh. The truth was a doozy and now Colt had to deal with that. Everything hadn't worked out fine at all. Jocelyn was gone. A baby, secretly conceived with another man's biological contribution, was without his mother. And his father would now look at his son's blue eyes and know they weren't his, after all.

She sent up a silent prayer of thanks that Colt was an intense person because he'd made it clear, with all the intensity burning inside him, that the news hadn't changed anything for him. Ryder was his son no matter what.

So maybe everything had worked out fine. Or would. With time.

He picked up his mug and took a long sip, leaning a bit closer now that he could without a baby on his lap. "Ava, there's something I *would* like to know."

She bit her lip. "Okay."

"Why wouldn't you promise not to tell me?"

She glanced out the window, the snow coming down harder now. She tried to focus on the snowflakes and not the memory of the morning Jocelyn had revealed her secret. "A few reasons.

Jocelyn blurted out the truth just a few days after he was born. She probably wasn't planning on telling me, either. But maybe the hormones and giving birth and the craziness of those first few magical, scary days of brand-new motherhood made her vulnerable and she told me."

She glanced at him and he was looking at her so intently. It was so strange to have such personal information about him, about his life, that he had no idea about. This wealthy, powerful CEO. But Colt Dawson was really just a man with a beating heart.

"At first I assumed you'd gone that route together—the fertility clinic, donor sperm," she continued. "But when she explained that she'd done it secretly and wasn't ever going to tell you, it just felt so… I'm not even sure of the word. But wrong, for sure."

He nodded, uneasy, she could tell, and looked over at Ryder, fast asleep.

"I like his pj's," she said, thinking a change of subject was in order. She smiled at the World's Greatest Nephew across his blue-and-white footies. "Gift from your sister?"

He nodded. "I told Haley about all this, by the way. She happened to come over just when I found the letter."

Ava pictured the pretty young woman, same blue eyes as her brother, but with long honey-brown hair. Ava used to stop into the Bear Ridge Diner a couple of times a week for lunch or to pick up soup and pie for dinner, and Haley, a waitress there, was always so warm. "I've met her a few times."

"Whoa," he said, gazing out the window. "When did that happen?"

She looked out, the snow coming down at a good clip now. "We're expecting half a foot."

"I was so out of my mind when I left my house that I didn't give the coming storm a thought," he said. "I passed an inn in downtown Prairie Hills on the way here. I'll book a room for the night since there's no way I'm driving back with Ryder in this."

"You're welcome to stay here," she said before she could think about it. "I have two extra bed-rooms and like I said, the basic necessities for Ryder. I have a bassinet, an infant swing and even changing necessities—diapers and ointment, all that stuff. I went a little nuts buying him newborn pj's and socks and caps, but, of course, none of that will fit him anymore."

She rarely went into that guest room. She could barely handle twenty seconds in there before she was socked with memories. Her former fiancé breaking up with her two days before their wedding. Then how Jocelyn had used it against her for why Ava wouldn't promise not to tell Colt the truth about Ryder.

"If you're sure," he said. "I can take care of some of the problems I noticed before the snow gets heavy. The barn door hinge. A piece of the fencing."

That she desperately needed his help was an understatement. Aunt Iris had been down to nothing in her bank account; in fact, it had been overdrawn. Ava had settled up what she needed to but she'd been a preschool teacher before this and hadn't been rolling in money herself. There was very little available to pay for repairs. If she wanted to be able to put on the Christmas festival, which would remind folks about the ranch and promote the spring camps, clubs and classes she intended to hold this spring, she wouldn't look a gift alpaca in the mouth. This was the only way to get the ranch back to at least decent shape.

"I'd appreciate your help, Colt. I'll be honest. I *need* your help. But I don't want you to feel obligated. Like I said, I'll tell you whatever you want to know. I'm just afraid of revealing what you don't *need* to know."

"I owe you," he said. "For *not* promising. For giving her reason to start that letter to you. I never would have known the truth otherwise. I always want the truth."

Truth, truth, truth. The word echoed in her head. He'd asked why she hadn't made that promise and she'd been honest when she said there were a few reasons. She just didn't plan to share the big one. Hopefully he wouldn't bring it up again.

But she had the rest of the day and *all* night to go here with Colt Dawson.

Chapter Four

"I'll get our bags from the truck," he said, standing up. "I didn't know how long we'd have to be here, so I brought the basics. Will you watch Ryder for a minute?" He'd put the little guy down for a proper nap in the bassinet in the guest room, then go take care of the barn hinge and the broken fence. Physical work would help clear his head. Being outside on this ranch would work whatever magic it could. Every muscle felt tight.

She smiled and stood up. "Sure."

Her whole face had lit up, and for a moment he couldn't take his eyes off her. Ava was very pretty, objectively, with her delicate features and soft, silky blond hair down her shoulders, the big hazel eyes. She'd looked sad and worried the entire time he'd been here. But right now, there was a sparkle to her. It hit him how much she must have missed Ryder, how much she'd lost, too.

On his way to the car, he got pelted by snow. He watched the alpacas for a moment, not sure if they needed to come in or not. He knew cattle and sheep from his summers on ranches, but he didn't know a thing about alpacas. He'd get Ryder settled, then help her bring them inside the barn and whatever else needed doing. Another glance around told him a lot.

Back inside, he found Ava standing by the window, holding Ryder, pointing at the tricolored alpaca who was still standing off to the side. The lone wolf.

"That's Star," she said to Ryder, swaying gently. "She's a keep-to-herself sort just like my aunt Iris was who left me this ranch. But I can tell Star likes me. She nuzzles my hand when I give her a treat."

"What do alpacas like to eat?" he asked.

She whirled around as if she hadn't heard him come in, but maybe she hadn't. They *both* had a lot on their minds. "Well, they're mostly pasture fed and have supplemental pellets and hay. But they like little pieces of apples and carrots."

"Do they need to come in?" he asked.

"In about a half hour," she said, glancing out. "They like the snow. But not heavy snow." She looked at Ryder, a hand rubbing his back. "He got fussy in his baby seat so I took him out. Figured I'd introduce him to the gals," she added, nodding at the alpacas.

"I'll take him," he said, reaching out. Her face fell a bit as if she didn't want to give him up. He was right about how much she'd missed Ryder, what the baby meant to her. He dropped his arms. "Or you could lead the way to the guest room."

She gave something of a smile, then headed up the stairs, cooing to Ryder before stopping at the only closed door.

Colt eyed the narrow hallway, painted that awful dark pink. It certainly wasn't fresh paint, so clearly Ava hadn't chosen the color.

"My aunt Iris loved pink. I like it, too, but not *this* much. I'll get around to redoing it once the bigger stuff is taken care of."

"I can paint it for you tomorrow morning. If the roads clear, I can head into town and get some supplies."

She turned to face him, her hand on the doorknob. "You really don't need to do anything, Colt. All those supplies, including nonpink paint, are in the basement and shed. I'll get to it one day."

"You've already got a lot to do just taking care of the alpacas and running this place. It must have been some steep learning curve."

"You have no idea," she said.

He pictured her out here alone in August, standing in the barn in sneakers because she didn't own boots meant for a ranch. Having no idea where to start, what to do. Grieving her friendship. Her relationship with Ryder. The loss of her aunt. And so isolated out here, fifteen miles from the nearest neighbor as far as he could see and thirty from town. And then just when she was three months into being an alpaca rancher, in the rhythm, he'd called with the news that Jocelyn was gone.

He'd never forget her intake of breath. The silence. The sob that he'd heard wrenched from her, deep inside. The conversation had been short and he'd told her about the arrangements but before he could even ask if she wanted to speak or read a poem or hymn at the service, she'd said goodbye.

Had to have been a really rough time, from the argument with Jocelyn to right now.

There'd been a fiancé at one point, he remembered. A couple of years ago. Colt and Jocelyn had gone to the small engagement party at a restaurant, but he'd excused himself so often to deal with calls from the office about fires big and small that he'd barely gotten to talk to the fiancé or Ava. There were a few dinners out with them, too, but it was always the same story, Colt called away. Making Godfrey and Dawson more important than anyone else.

He sighed.

And wondered what happened with Ava's fiancé. If he was remembering right, the guy had called off the wedding the week of, maybe even just a couple of days beforehand.

She'd certainly been through her share of hard knocks.

"Well, for someone who's only had a few months' experience working with alpacas," he said, "it's clear you're doing great with them. They look very healthy and well cared for."

Her face lit up. "I'm so glad you said that. When I first got here, I asked the vet to come out once a week to check them over just to give me peace of mind. I drove the woman nuts. She charged me time and a half and a promise of a skein of their fleece for each visit when I get all that going again. Well worth it."

His vision of her in her sneakers, not knowing a thing about the alpacas she'd inherited, was clearly spot-on. "I probably would have done the same," he said. "It's been fourteen years since I've been a cowboy. Peace of mind is priceless."

"I'll take it where I can get it," she said, opening the door. "It's not always easy to find." She glanced at him for a second, then stepped inside the room. "This is the guest room. Everything you need for Ryder for at least a week is in here," she added.

He was grateful it wasn't pink like the hallway. The walls were a soothing shade of off-white, a big round rug in gradating shades of blue on the wood floor. A frilly bassinet with blue ruffles was by the window, a wood changing table with a white pad on top.

"I also have bottles and infant formula," she added, "but probably not the right age range at this point."

He pointed to the bag slung over his shoulder. "I'm all set there. I learned to always carry a supply for a day or two of whatever he needs." A few times over the month, he'd been out with Ryder in town and didn't have what he needed and had to go scrambling in stores, not sure of size or preferred brands. One shopper, a man with two kids in tow, had said on a snort, *When the Sunday dad has to take junior out.*

Colt had wanted to deck him. But, of course, the guy hadn't been wrong. That was Colt. Sunday dad. He'd made sure ever since that Ryder's bag had the basics always packed and fresh stuff added, his bottle.

She headed over to the bassinet with Ryder. "Will he wake up when I transfer him?"

"Probably," he said. "He does any time I try when he's already asleep. But I'm not good at any of this." He'd never seen a face go from peaceful to red and scrunched like Ryder Dawson's when he attempted to put him down for a nap in a crib. He'd read something in his fatherhood primer about making sure the baby was ready for the bassinet, fully tired, full belly, changed, cooed to. But even with all that, he'd never gotten the timing right. Ryder always seemed untired or overtired.

"Any of what?" Ava asked, gently caressing Ryder's hair.

"Fatherhood. I try, but I seem to get it wrong three-quarters of the time."

"Get what wrong? I mean, exactly?"

Everything. Every. Little. Thing. "Putting him down just right like my cousin Ford does with his own baby so he doesn't wake up," Colt explained. "The way my sister does when she comes over and she doesn't have much child care experience. She just picked it up from having a nephew. I've been Ryder's sole parent for a month and I can't figure out if he's hungry or tired or what or how not to wake him up." Why was he saying all this? He clamped his mouth shut.

"Well, Jocelyn probably didn't give you much

of a chance to learn to be a dad," she said. "She was pretty territorial. When I came to visit in the maternity wing, she didn't like anyone holding him, even me."

He nodded, remembering that himself. "I guess I thought fatherhood would be more instinctive."

He'd been an expectant father at the same time Ford was, so the two had talked a lot about just how little they knew what to *expect*, despite the googling and reading. *My brothers and sister told me you meet the new little person the second they're born and that's it*, Ford had said, *you fall madly in love and it's like you've been a father forever. Yeah, maybe it's a little awkward at first, diapering and bathing and holding the bottle just so, but the bond is so powerful it guides you.*

Colt had felt that bond, right there in the delivery room, and it was stronger than ever now, despite what he knew—in spite of what he knew, too. He *loved* Ryder. Loved him in his bones, with every cell of his body. He should be a more natural father at this point. He should be able to take care of his own baby without so much damned help.

"You seem like a great father to me," she said. "Clearly devoted."

He looked at her and could hug her. He didn't realize how badly he needed this, not from the usual support system but from this one person who knew so much about him, stuff he didn't want to contemplate or wonder about. There was no pretending with Ava, no point in it. "I appreciate that."

She gave his hand a fast squeeze and he wanted to hold on just a bit longer. "Well, let's see. Hopefully he'll go down without a peep."

Colt watched her gently lay Ryder into the bassinet. The baby stirred and turned his head, then was still, his chest rising up and down, up and down.

"It's just me, I guess," Colt said with half a smile.

But truth be told, he was stung and it was his own damned fault. *You outsourced care of your baby to your relatives and you wonder why you can't do the simplest thing right when it comes to taking care of your son?* He once saw one of his VPs, in too much of a hurry at a meeting to call his administrative assistant, actually trying to make a copy of a one-page document—and failing miserably. The paper was upside down. Then backward. Then got stuck in the machine.

That was Colt with his own child.

She smiled back. "Give yourself time. It's only been a month." She headed over to the dresser and turned on one of the two baby monitors, then took the other and handed it to him.

Well, it had been *four months* since that was how old Ryder was. Colt was four months late. Just one month on his own. Those first three months should have made him a pro for suddenly being a single father, but there he'd been, on an airplane. On a call.

He shook his head. *Just get back to right now. Focus on now.* He looked at the monitor. "You really do have everything."

"After my…argument with Jocelyn, I never expected to see him in this room, using any of this. I know it's not under the best circumstances, so I hope it's okay that I'm so glad he's here." She peered into the bassinet, and the look on her face, the love, the relief, truly touched him, then hurried from the room, and he followed into the pink hallway.

"I understand, Ava. He's part of your best friend, even if things were strained between you two."

Her eyes welled with tears. "We never spoke after that argument, Colt. And then she died."

He set down the baby monitor on the hall table and reached for Ava, and she came right into his embrace. He wrapped his arms around her in a hug. "I know how you feel." That he and Jocelyn hadn't argued the morning of the accident was no small relief.

She looked up at him, swiping under eyes. She didn't respond but he could see what she was thinking: *Yeah, I'll bet you do.*

"You okay?" he asked gently. Of course she wasn't, though. As they'd admitted to each other earlier, neither of them was. And it might be a while for even *half-okay*.

"I'm okay," she said in a shaky voice. "I'll be okay, anyway," she added more firmly.

He squeezed her hand, then picked up the monitor and practically ran for the stairs.

Because holding Ava had felt too good. Necessary. He could have stood there for hours just holding on to her. She knew things. She understood. There was no need to talk. The comfort in that was beyond anything he'd experienced the last weeks.

She hurried past him. "I'll show you the rest of the house quickly," she said, her voice a bit squeaky.

And he knew she'd felt the same way.

As Ava led Colt on the tour, which didn't take long in a fifteen-hundred-square-foot home, she was relieved when he said the house had good bones. She'd needed to hear that. A stamp of approval, of some type of assurance that the place wasn't going to fall down around her or on her head as she slept.

It felt like the hug he'd given her. Warm and comforting and just what she needed. It had been two years since she'd been in a man's arms. And Colt Dawson was tall and strong. For a tall woman, she'd felt enveloped by him, his strength and…yes, maleness. She could have stayed in that embrace a while. All day, maybe. Out here on the Prairie Hills Alpaca Ranch, the adorable, sweet alpacas didn't hug back.

"It's well-built," Colt added with a nod as they stopped near the front door, thankfully shaking her out of her thoughts. "Just a few areas need a little work and the place could use a fresh coat of paint, but the house seems sound."

"It was originally a sheep farm going generations back in the same family but it ended up abandoned for a while, and Iris got it cheap. I read that in some paperwork I found in her office. She had the house fixed up best she could on a budget, the barn, too, and turned it into an alpaca farm. It was all her. I feel connected to her here. Despite having had no experience on a ranch or with alpacas, from the first day I still felt like I *belonged* here. Isn't that crazy?"

"Not crazy at all. That's how I feel every time I'm on a ranch. My parents weren't rodeo people and my dad couldn't stand animals, let alone livestock, so I didn't grow up around horses or ranches. But we'd go to the county fair out in the country, and when I'd see the horses and the pigs and sheep vying for prizes, the cowboys working, I'd feel something in my bones. A rightness. And the first time I stepped foot on a working cattle ranch, I *knew*. That was my path, my road, my future."

She smiled, imagining him as a kid watching the pigs in the mud, the sheep baaing, the majestic horses, the cowboys doing their work, and feeling that spark.

"The entire two-hour drive here," he continued, "my knuckles were practically white on the steering wheel, every muscle in my body tense, my mind going really bad places. No idea what to expect when I got here, what you'd say, if you'd even say anything. And the second I drove through the two brick pillars to the property and saw the big red barn and pastures and the grazing alpacas, I felt just enough sense of peace to catch my breath."

She could imagine how hellish the drive had been for him. Finding that letter and then coming to see its intended recipient, not sure if he'd get answers.

Now they were going to bring in the alpacas and she'd give him a quick tour of the barn. She opened the hall closet door and handed him his coat, then slipped into her down jacket and put on her wool hat. "I remember Jocelyn telling me you once wanted to be a rancher but that your dad set your head straight on that."

"I had my heart set on having my own ranch, cattle and sheep, but my path ended up being on a different route. Jocelyn always said if she met me as a rancher we wouldn't have ever gone on that first date."

Jocelyn had mentioned that once, so casually with a roll of her eyes and a *Thank God his father was able to talk sense into him or Colt and I wouldn't have had a first date. And you and I would not be having coffee right now in my gorgeous kitchen in this gorgeous house.* Times when Ava would think her best friend was incredibly materialistic and obsessed with *fancy*, she'd remember how Jocelyn grew up. An orphaned foster kid on a farm where she was very lonely and did not find comfort in livestock.

People were complicated. Her aunt Iris had been—all the more so because despite wanting nothing to do with what little family she had, she'd had the hospital get in touch with Ava and she'd been able to come for the last two days of her great-aunt's life.

But *complicated* was Jocelyn's middle name.

"Yeah, Jocelyn was not a country gal," Ava said.

"Nope." He put on his cowboy hat and walked over to the windows alongside the door. "So how do we get the alpacas to the barn? You attach a lead?"

She shook her head. "I have an easier way."

As he put on his leather gloves, she couldn't help but stare at him for a second. She really couldn't remember ever seeing Colt Dawson in a cowboy hat before today. He looked like the picture of a cowboy now. The man she'd remembered in suits and expensive-looking shoes was gone. This new Colt was sexy, she thought.

It felt weird thinking of him that way, so she opened the door and they headed out to the pasture. She could see him putting his hand in his coat pocket a couple of times, clearly making sure the baby monitor was still there, ready to alert if Ryder started crying. There hadn't been a sound from him since they'd left the nursery five minutes ago.

"You use a herding dog?" he asked, glancing around.

She shook her head. "Alpacas don't love dogs, so no four-legged herders here. Just me." She reached into her pocket and held up a slice of apple. "Treats!" she called out, and all six alpacas turned their fuzzy heads her way. "Treats!"

He laughed as they all slowly made their way to the gate of the pasture. He ran ahead to open it, the snow falling around him while Ava dashed back to the side door of the barn and opened it. They meandered right to her, each stopping for their bit of apple and a pat on their furry necks before heading inside.

"That's something," he said, nodding. "It's like having a ranch hand and herding dog in one baggie of apple slices."

"Yup. My aunt left me a few pages of instruction with some sticky notes about how to do the basics. Her tips and tricks were everything. I did a lot of my own research when I first got there, but without Iris's notes about how to get Cookie to stop spitting when she got mad about something or not to panic if I saw all the alpacas lying like the dead in their pasture—it's just their way of sunbathing—I'd have been lost."

"Kind of like me with Ryder's schedule. But even though I follow it to the T or try to, I'm just kind of not great at it."

"Maybe you're too hard on yourself. Expecting perfection or something. Or expecting Ryder to be or react the way numbers do when you're crunching them at work. Babies are all about the gray and gradations."

He smiled. "Yeah, Ryder does seem to be his own baby."

She laughed. "Good. Already a trailblazer."

His smile faded. Fast.

"I say something wrong?"

"My dad hoped I'd have a son, specifically a son, as heir to the Godfrey and Dawson lineup of co-CEOs. That's what he expected of me and the timing made it happen. He asked me on his deathbed to take over for him, and how could I say no? All my plans, my dreams to have my own ranch? Gone like that," he said with a snap of his fingers. "But when he laid out that life for my son before he was even born, I saw red."

Oh, Colt, she thought. She knew a little of this from Jocelyn but not the details. "And what if you'd had a girl?"

"My father was old-school in a bad way. Traditional in a bad way. If my sister had been the older one, I really wonder what he would have done, if he'd have asked her to take over for him."

"Would she have? I know I've met her a couple times but I don't know her."

"Haley? No way. She would have said, 'Dad, I love you, but I'm going to open my own restaurant someday and be a Michelin-starred chef.' She works her butt off as a waitress at the Bear Ridge Diner and has learned more about the business that way than she ever expected. She wants to open a pasta joint next year and I plan to help fund her dream. She just doesn't know that yet."

Ava smiled. "God, I love pasta. I could go for a big plate of spaghetti carbonara and garlic bread right now."

"Me, too," he said.

"Count on it for dinner, then. I'm pretty sure I have all the ingredients."

He smiled, his whole expression changing. Softening.

"Well," she said, forcing her eyes off his face. "I'd better spread out the rest of the straw." She practically ran to the wheelbarrow to give herself some room from him.

"I'll help," he said, coming right over and

standing close as he grabbed a heap of straw. She directed him where to put it and he got a nuzzle from Cookie, who loved attention.

"She likes me," he said, patting her neck. "So soft. I wasn't expecting that."

"Alpaca fleece is so much softer than wool. And warmer. My toes love my alpaca socks, especially in winter."

They finished spreading the hay, then stood back and watched the alpacas. Ava adored them. They all had long necks, some skinny necks, some not, some with sideways ears, some not. Star was standing in her own little area, as was her way, Cookie and Pecan sitting together, kushing, she'd learned it was called, kind of like hens, very close together. Princess was testing her favorite spot to make sure it was thick enough. She was like the Princess in the *Princess and the Pea*. And Lorelai and Rory were standing facing each other, just kind of looking at each other, maybe having some kind of mother-daughter telepathic conversation.

"They all get along?" he asked as they stood just outside the pen.

"Yup. Those two," she said, pointing to the black-and-white ones, "are mother and daughter.

And those all-white ones are seniors—eighteen years old."

She knew they must miss Iris and wonder where she was and who this newbie interloper was. Ava had worked through her grief and disappointment over missing out ever knowing her great-aunt by taking to the alpacas. She'd explained the family history, what little she knew, and that Iris, for whatever reason, had closed herself off, estranged herself from her family, and devoted herself to the alpacas. They must have brought her so much happiness, Ava thought, watching them. Sweet and gentle, asking for so little, just pasture and hay and water, alpaca buddies and the occasional treat.

"So the main purpose of the ranch is what?" he asked, watching as Cookie gave Pecan a little nudge.

"Alpaca fleece. Once a year, every summer, the alpacas are shorn, and their fleece is turned into fiber for all sorts of projects. Knitting, pillows, blankets, comforters. My aunt used to handmake her own duvets and pillows and sell them to stores all across the state, hotels, too. And her yarns and knitting projects were also carried in local stores. She did some breeding, too, but apparently she wasn't well the past couple years, and she stopped doing much except the basic care of the alpacas. The ranch got kind of run-down, as you see." Tears poked the backs of Ava's eyes. "I wish she'd gotten in touch. I could have helped, or tried, anyway."

He put an arm around her and gave her a squeeze.

"I'm sorry," she said, wiping under her eyes and looking up at him. "You're the one whose life just got upended and here I am, sobbing on your shirt every five minutes."

"It's more than okay," he said, his strong arms so comforting around her. "If you'd known, you would have been here. She must have known that because she did get in touch at the end, she wanted you there to say goodbye. And she left this place to you. From what you've told me, this ranch meant everything to her. It was her life."

She could feel herself brightening. Yes. He was right. Iris was a loner like Star, plain and simple, and she'd estranged herself for her own reasons. Maybe Ava would find out why as she started going through her aunt's things. So far, she hadn't had the time or energy.

But right now, she let herself have this hug— she *needed* this kindness like air. She'd been so alone for the past four months.

He looked at her, so much compassion and warmth in his eyes, and she'd never felt closer to anyone than in that moment. He looked away fast, out the open double windows along the barn wall. They watched the snow fall for a few seconds, then Ava closed both wooden doors and latched them. "Well, the gals are settled for now. We can head back in."

They ran to the house, shaking the snow off their hats on the big mat inside the front door.

She smiled as she took off her hat and coat. "Always feels so good to come into the warm house after the cold and snow."

"You still have straw in your hair," he said, reaching for it.

She tried to ignore how her neck and shoulders still tingled at his touch. "I find straw inside my shirt often, too. Sometimes I think the alpacas take turns sneaking up behind me, giggling, and pick some up with their mouths and drop it down the back of my shirt."

He laughed. "They probably do."

It was good to hear him laugh. But a little cry came from the monitor in his hand and his smile kind of faded. "I'll just go check on Ryder. I know I'm supposed to give him a moment to self-soothe but I can't seem to ignore a cry."

"Which makes you devoted to him," she said. "It'll all come, Colt. Feeling comfortable enough to let a cry go. Knowing it's okay. Give yourself time to learn. Fatherhood, taking care of a baby— it's a huge job."

"I *want* the job," he said. "More than I ever realized. I just didn't know I'd be doing it on my own." He let out a breath and took off his coat, his shoulders so broad. She wondered if she'd be noticing his shoulders if he hadn't hugged her upstairs earlier. Probably. Colt was hard not to notice. Everything about him.

He was quiet for a moment, then said, "Well, I'll go check on him."

She nodded and watched him go up the steps. Before, she'd needed some space between them but now she just wanted to wrap her arms around him, assure him he had this, that he'd be the father he needed to be.

He was back in a few minutes. "Sound asleep. I want to go take care of the near fence before the snow gets bad, but I do want to know something, Ava."

"Okay," she said, bracing herself.

"Why was it so important to Jocelyn that I not know she was artificially inseminated? I mean, she'd never even brought up the possibility of a fertility clinic or alternate routes to getting pregnant."

"She was afraid you'd say no. That bloodlines would matter to you because they were important in your family—your father and grandfather, the Dawsons."

He glanced away. "I tried to talk to her about my father and what he wanted for me and what I wanted for myself. But she didn't like talking about that. I think she was afraid I'd quit Godfrey and Dawson and buy some cattle and sheep and make good on my dream."

"Why didn't you?" she asked.

"How do you go back on a deathbed promise?" he asked. "You know what a promise means, Ava. You must take promises very seriously if you wouldn't even promise Jocelyn not to tell me I wasn't Ryder's father."

She nodded slowly.

"You still haven't told me why, though."

"Maybe later. Over dinner," she said. "It's… not a straightforward answer." She really didn't want to talk about any of that. Then again, maybe talking about it would help. She'd had no one to talk to about what happened with Jocelyn. Just the alpacas.

Now it was his turn to nod.

"Are you taking off work until the new year?" she asked.

"No. I force myself not to go into the office on weekends now that it's just Ryder and me. But tomorrow is Monday. I'm expected. I have three meetings scheduled."

She raised an eyebrow. "Expected by whom? You're the CEO."

"Well, co-CEO. And it's a big job."

"You said the same about fatherhood."

He didn't respond for a second. "I found the letter and packed an overnight bag for me and Ryder just in case I'd need to stick around a couple days. So while I'm expected, I'm not planning on going in till at least midweek."

She tilted her head. "You think by Wednesday you'll magically be able to focus on anything but the letter and Ryder and fatherhood?"

"I have responsibilities, Ava."

"Yes, I have no doubt. But you also have a co-CEO, Godfrey Jr. Jr. You have people who work for you. Delegate, Colt. Take this time for yourself and your son. You're already here and the roads will likely be awful for a while anyway. It's supposed to snow all week."

Things were rough right now for him. And it

was Christmas. Didn't he see the timing made it actually possible to take off a couple of weeks?

"I'll get started on the fence," he said, completely ignoring what she'd said. "If you don't mind keeping an ear on Ryder? I don't mean to assume."

"And I didn't mean to overstep," she said.

He looked directly at her, his blue eyes holding so many different emotions she couldn't pick one out. "It's fine. Someone has to be straight with me, right?"

She smiled, not expecting that response. "I'm glad you see it that way. And I'd be happy to keep an ear on Ryder. If there's one thing I do know a lot about, it's little kids since I used to work at a day care."

He put his coat and hat back on. "Be back in about a half hour."

She missed him the moment the door shut behind him.

lyn's past and background and hang-ups
her extremely fearful of not having any
ties to anyone. She'd been alone in the
It was probably the real reason she never
Colt to know that he wasn't blood-related
er. Jocelyn had believed in the deepest
f her heart that it *would* matter, no matter
Colt would *say*. So the promise had been
ant to her.

Ava couldn't bring herself to promise.
never going to come up, he'll never
t, so just promise, dammit, Jocelyn had
ed.

n't make that promise, Ava had said, still
hear the anguish in her voice. *What if*
some kind of medical emergency? I don't
ow or why it would ever come up but if
nd he asked me directly, how could I lie
ace?

ous, Jocelyn had shaken her head, slowly.
just a bitter... I'm done with you...

t if she *had* promised and Colt had shown
way he had, demanding answers. Would
back on her word?

she wasn't bitter about not being able to
ids. She did wish she could get pregnant,
nedical issue had made that impossible

Chapter Five

Ava was going up the stairs to peek in on Ryder when she heard a cry come from the monitor. She went into the nursery and over to the bassinet. The baby stared up at her with big blue eyes. He was so darn cute.

She could hardly believe he was here, this precious baby she thought she'd never see again. She carefully slipped one hand under his neck before lifting him up and brought him over to the changing pad. He gave his legs a little kick, making some gurgling sounds. He looked happy. She changed his diaper and sprinkled on some cornstarch, then got him back into his cotton one-piece pj's and scooped him up in her arms.

"Oh, how sweet you are," she said, snuggling him as she sat down in the rocker by the window.

Do not think about Jocelyn, do not think about Jocelyn, she chanted a few more times. But, of course, with her friend's baby in her arms, how could she not?

Which brought the sharp voice, the accusations that stabbed at her heart.

You're just bitter that you can't have kids at all, Jocelyn had snapped. *That's why you won't promise. You hate that I'm pregnant. You liked it better when I was crying every month when I got my period.*

Just. Like. You, Jocelyn had added for the kill.

Ava closed her eyes, letting it come, all Jocelyn had said, Ava cut to the core.

And then more memories joined in.

I'm sorry, Ava, her former fiancé had said two years ago. *I thought I could do this but I can't marry a woman who can't have children. Bloodlines matter to my family.*

He'd called off the wedding two days before it was scheduled. And it was Jocelyn who'd been there for her, spiriting her off to an inn where they'd cried and watched movies and ate ice cream. *You'll find the right guy one day*, her best friend had assured her. *And he won't give a flying rat's tush about bloodlines. Bloodlines don't matter.*

Bloodlines *didn't* matter. But Jocelyn had believed that bloodlines would matter to *Colt*. Her entire reason for keeping what she'd done a secret was because of that.

Maybe DNA did matter t
said otherwise, he'd also said
son and he had become like
childhood he'd had.

No. She'd barely spent twen
the man and even she knew th
If bloodlines were important
have accepted the truth the wa

It was the lie, the betrayal, th
the truth itself.

She felt a yank on her hair.
thought, trying to gently extric
hair from Ryder's firm grip. Sl
tle tickle and he laughed, whic

"Everything's gonna be oka
to him. "I'm going to be okay.
right?"

Ryder stared at her with his
those first few scrunched-face
she'd thought he looked like his
Jocelyn had blurted out the tru
he didn't look like Colt Dawso
the coloring.

I could have a child, she'd sa
Adoption.

Jocelyn had shrugged. *Wel
to be my blood relation.*

Joc
made
blood
world.
wante
to Ry
parts
what
impo
Ar
It'
find
screa
I c
able
there
know
it did
in his
Fu
You're
Wl
up the
she g
An
have
but a

in her early twenties. Ava had worked for years at a day care, for heaven's sake. She certainly didn't begrudge others children. She loved kids, all ages. At Bear Ridge Day Care, there had been so many different kinds of families. Adoptive, biological, grandparents as legal guardians. One didn't make a family more than the other.

Ryder let out a little babbling noise and Ava shook off her thoughts, forcing her mind on the baby. She got up, loving the soft weight of him in her arms, and walked over to the bookshelf, picking out a children's book and sitting back down. She'd distract herself with a story about a piglet who didn't like mud and refused to get dirty. "Pauline the piglet wouldn't last a day at Prairie Hills Alpaca Ranch," she said to Ryder.

He batted at the book, maybe looking at the beautiful illustrations but probably not. She read him the story, which was adorable, then got another one. When she heard the front door open, she took Ryder downstairs, Colt coming in as she was halfway down.

He walked over and caressed his son's head. "I fixed the fence, but there are two more that need attention. Plus the barn needs some work."

"Why do you look so happy about that?" she

asked. His cheeks were a bit red from the cold, but his eyes were bright and twinkling.

"It's good, hard work. Physical. Requires tools, hands," he said, holding them up. "And there's not a soul around. Just the sound of the treetops moving in the wind. Every time I look up, there's nothing but sky and land and mountains."

"I always lived in town in Bear Ridge, but I love it out here, too. There's just such a peace."

He nodded. "It's done wonders for me already. I checked on the alpacas, by the way. They're just hanging out." He glanced at his watch. "And it's time for this guy's dinner. I'll go make up his bottle. If you don't mind hanging on to him."

She could hold Ryder forever. "Not at all. I read him two stories upstairs. He likes piglets more than snails."

He laughed. "Thanks for watching him."

"Of course. And thanks for fixing that fence."

He smiled but stayed put, looking at Ryder, looking at her. Then he headed into the kitchen.

She stood there for a moment, overcome with *everything*. All the painful memories that had gone through her mind just a little while ago. Holding a baby. *This* baby. The way Colt Dawson had comforted her. The way she could talk to him. The way he'd come into her house just now.

The way she could hardly take her eyes off him.

Be careful, Ava, she warned herself. *You are overwhelmed and yes, lonely. But you want to talk complicated? You and Colt Dawson would be* very *complicated.*

Ryder let out a fussy whine and she gave him a little bounce, then took him over to the kitchen doorway.

"Look, sweets, there's your daddy, making your lunch."

Colt turned from where he stood at the counter with the bottle and shot them both a smile that went straight to her toes. The kitchen was big but he filled it up. She still wasn't quite used to seeing a man in her kitchen. In her house.

And he'd be staying here tonight.

"Perfect timing," he said. "You can check if his bottle is too hot." He squeezed out a bit on his finger and touched it. "Seems okay to me."

She stepped closer to him and he squeezed a drop on the back of her hand. "It's just right."

"I'm getting there," he said, holding out his arms.

She wasn't ready to give up this sweet bundle but handed him over, then followed Colt into the living room. He sat down on the tan sofa, settling Ryder against his arm. "You look very natural at this, Colt."

"Well, I was always pretty good at hiding how I'm really doing."

She took that in, just as he seemed to look a little uncomfortable at having said so much in one line.

"I'll go grab the playpen and baby swing from upstairs," she said. "You can set them up down here wherever you want."

But she stayed where she was, unable to take her eyes off Colt feeding his son. The tall, muscular man on her sofa giving the tiny baby in his World's Best Nephew pj's his bottle.

"So far, so good," Colt said, looking up at her for a second.

She knew in that moment she had feelings for Colt Dawson she shouldn't. They both needed something from the other—that was all that was going on here. She had information she needed. He knew his way around tools.

And had given her back a piece of her best friend.

And had held her when she cried.

And looked so handsome, so sexy sitting there with his baby that she couldn't take another moment.

"Be right back," she said.

She went back upstairs and after two trips up

and down, she had the foldable playpen and swing in the living room.

"What does it mean that he's pulling away even though there's some left," he asked, glancing up at her. "He's done? It's okay for him not to finish the bottle? I feel like I've asked this before. I know I have."

"It's okay," she said. "Or he might need to burp and then finish. Give that a try."

"I should know this." He shook his head. "I can run a corporation but not remember the most basic facts about feeding my child."

"You'll get there, Colt," she said. "You know how we were talking before about delegating? This is the one area you shouldn't delegate—the questions. You're asking because you're doing the work. And that's how you learn. Back at home, you said your family jumped in."

"And I let them," he said, giving Ryder's back gentle but firm pats.

Burp!

They both laughed.

"Big burp for a little boy," Colt said. "Now I'll see if he wants to finish the bottle."

She watched as he repositioned the baby, then put the bottle to his lips. Ryder turned away.

"Nope. He's done." He exhaled and brought

Ryder to his chest. "I'm not proud of this, Ava, but I think this was the first time I fed him."

She gaped at him. "Really?"

"The past month, someone was always around. Sleeping over, running to get Ryder, taking care of everything. My family kind of walked on eggshells around me. And I let them take care of Ryder. I let them do my job. And now I don't know what the hell I'm doing."

"You're further along than you think," she said.

He raised Ryder up in the air. "I think Ava's just being nice," he said to the baby.

She supposed she was. The man did have a ways to go. But he was trying.

And she was falling.

Colt glanced at his phone on the bedside table in the guest room. 1:42 a.m. He lay on his side in bed, propped up on an elbow, Ryder's bassinet right along the edge. He couldn't sleep, but that wasn't anything new. Of course, now he couldn't sleep because he was here, in Ava's house, and she was two doors down the pink hallway. He liked having Ryder beside him, watching him sleep.

Why hadn't he moved Ryder into his bedroom at home? Ryder had slept in the nursery as usual,

Colt in his bedroom, his sister or a cousin or cousin-in-law dashing into the nursery if the baby cried, ready for his 3:00 a.m. bottle. While he'd lain there, awake, staring at the ceiling, half of his king-size bed empty.

No one had suggested he move Ryder's crib or the bassinet into his bedroom and now he knew why. First of all, the thought hadn't even occurred to Colt and no doubt his family was aware of that. They knew he was out of his element and they helped. Now that a month had passed since he was a single parent, he also had no doubt his sister would sit him down for a talking-to. She had here and there, trying to get him to learn a thing or two about taking care of his own son, but hadn't been all that serious about it. There was some "poor Colt" in the whispers. And "he really doesn't know the basics." He thought he heard his cousins Ford and Rex talking about a class for new fathers. Of course, with a four-month-old, he was a completely new father. But maybe he'd ask about that class.

I need to be a better father, he said silently to Ryder, watching his chest rise and fall, rise and fall. He'd handled the baby's entire bedtime routine on his own tonight. A first.

Yeah, here's your medal. Congrats. Your kid is four months old.

It was a start, he reminded himself.

After dinner—Ava's spaghetti carbonara was delicious—she'd asked what Ryder's schedule was, typical bedtime, how long beforehand was bath time, how many stories, had he started tummy time yet, and Colt had been unable to answer any of that without having to look at the long list Jocelyn had typed up every month to account for the changes in development. Which had been upstairs in Ryder's bag in the guest room.

"No need to go grab the schedule," she'd said. "You can make one up yourself in your head right now. Based on the nap he took earlier and when he had his dinner bottle, you'll know how many hours till he's ready for bed. Maybe an hour beforehand, you can start bath time and stories."

You can start...

He'd given Ryder a bath once. Once. In four months. And yes, he should be able to figure out his son's schedule just by the last bottle, the last nap. Or by Ryder's yawns or cries. He needed to rely less on a this-is-going-to-happen-at-this-time list and more on his instincts. On Ryder himself.

And so he'd thrown him into the bedtime routine, determined to handle it on his own and do it right. Like the only other time he'd given Ryder a bath himself, there was too much water splashed on the counter and floor. The small sample of baby shampoo in Ryder's bag had come in handy, suds everywhere, including on Colt's face and shirt. Ava had popped her head in at that point, of course, and tried to hide that she was laughing, but burst forth. She'd gotten a flick of suds for that.

He'd then laid Ryder on the changing pad and since he'd noticed one of his little legs was a bit dry, he used some lotion. He'd gotten the diaper on right-side up and fresh pj's on, the baby smelling heavenly.

He'd read Ryder a story about a reindeer who didn't like the snow, but his eyes had started drooping before the end. The transfer into the bassinet hadn't gone well the first two times, but the third was the ole charm. By then, Colt was exhausted but he'd had a few more repairs he wanted to take care of in the house and so had gone downstairs. Ava had made herself scarce and when he'd realized he'd missed her company, he went looking for her. But as he'd headed up the stairs to the dark pink hallway, he'd actually run right into her, his hands reaching out to her shoulders to right her, and he'd realized he'd needed to see her, to be near her.

Dangerous.

They'd made some awkward small talk and when he said he'd probably turn in for the night and asked which room was his, she looked at him like he had four heads and said the guest room—where Ryder was sleeping.

"Of course," he'd said fast. As though he'd always known they'd be sharing a room.

And now he was inches away from his boy, smelling that wonderful baby smell.

"I still think you look like me," he whispered, reaching out a finger to touch Ryder's hair. "I don't care what that letter said."

He lay like that for a good five minutes, just watching the baby sleep, his chest feeling warm and full in a good way. He felt so at peace then, all right with his world in this moment, that he felt himself drifting off and pulled the great comforter up around his shoulders and settled his head onto the soft pillow.

And then all hell broke loose. Ryder let out a bloodcurdling shriek to the point that Colt jumped out of bed, almost bumping into the bassinet. Colt reached in to pick him up, but Ryder wouldn't stop crying.

He paced the room, bouncing, swaying, rocking, shushing, rubbing his back. Nothing worked. Ryder wouldn't stop shrieking.

Where was Ava? Shouldn't she be running in?

He waited, hoping to hear her footsteps, but he didn't.

Maybe he couldn't hear over Ryder's shrieks. His face was all red and he was screaming bloody murder.

"It's okay," Colt said, holding him vertically, giving his back little pats. "Let's walk around the room some more. Maybe you have gas? You need to burp? You had a nightmare?" Did babies have nightmares?

Maybe about dads like him, who didn't know what the hell they were doing.

Where was Ava? Fast asleep like she should be.

Ryder was still crying. He tried to remember what the different cries meant, but how could he think over the bloodcurdling screams? He left the room and headed down the hall toward Ava's room, the change in scenery not making his son any happier. As if this dark pink would make anyone smile.

He put his ear to Ava's door. Not a sound.

Except for Ryder's screams. How was she sleeping through this?

He knocked. "Ava? You awake?"

Ryder scrunched up his face and cried. And cried. And cried.

The door opened. Ava was in a T-shirt and leggings, her blond hair loose past her shoulders. "Hi," she said with a gentle smile.

Had she been wearing earplugs? "You must be a really heavy sleeper. I'm sorry for waking you."

"Oh, I wasn't sleeping. I was actually going through one of my aunt's old boxes, looking into her past."

He tilted his head, Ryder still crying. If she could hear it—and honestly, how could she not have—why hadn't she come?

"You've got this," she said with a firm nod.

He frowned. "Well, I don't because I can't get him to stop crying."

"Have you tried laying him down on the bed and gently pumping his little legs like he was riding a bike? That helps get rid of gas. Give that a try."

The door gently closed. In his face.

Interesting. Not in a good way, either.

Scowling and honestly kind of nervous, Colt hurried back to his room and laid Ryder down on the bed. He stopped crying for a second, then went right back to it.

"Like you're riding a bike," Colt repeated. He gently took each of Ryder's feet and moved his legs like he was riding a bike.

The cries got weaker.

The cries stopped.

Hallelujah!

Ryder's eyes were droopy but open. Colt scooped him up and swayed back and forth a little, singing a made-up lullaby about Wyoming winters. The little eyes got heavier. And heavier.

Here goes everything, Colt thought, settling Ryder back in the bassinet as gently as possible, praying he wouldn't start screeching again.

He didn't. But his eyes didn't close completely, either.

Colt slid back into bed, lying on his side facing the baby. "I could tell you a story. Once upon a time, there was an alpaca named Star. Star was a loner type. Kept to herself. She ate the pasture grass by herself. Sunbathed in the Wyoming winter sunshine by herself. Took naps by herself. Even though there were five other alpaca friends in the big pasture and their pen in the barn, Star liked to be alone." He peered at Ryder. Eyes were closed—yes! "But the other alpacas needed a fifth alpaca for their alpaca crawl race," he continued in more of a whisper. "At first she said no but then she saw how sad they were and so she said yes. Well, with Star joining the team, they won the race. And Star was part of the pack from then on."

"You got him to stop crying *and* just made up an adorable story?" Ava asked in a low voice.

He looked up and Ava was standing in the doorway. "Don't forget that he's sleeping again." Phew. That was intense.

"Told you, you had this," she said. "You did and then some."

Hardly. "If you hadn't mentioned the bike legs, I wouldn't have known to do that. Ryder would still be screaming like mad."

"You would have googled for how to get your baby to stop crying in the middle of the night. You would have found some ideas and tried them."

"How, with him crying his head off?"

"Isn't necessity the mother of invention? It's exactly why you told him a story made up on the spot. And it worked. He was still awake when you put him down but your story lulled him to sleep."

Huh. He supposed so. He was a little too used to everyone else taking care of Ryder.

She smiled at him, then came into the room and leaned down over the bassinet to give Ryder a kiss on his head. "See you later in the morning. The later morning. Which will probably be five o'clock."

She was so close. Suddenly all he wanted was to just sit and talk. Lie down and talk. He just didn't want her to leave.

But she gave him another soft smile and then was gone.

The good news was that when he lay back down and looked at Ryder, the baby was still asleep. Given everything that had happened with Ava today, Colt, on the other hand, wasn't going to sleep at all.

Chapter Six

The next morning, Ava was in the kitchen at 5:15 a.m., sitting at the table with coffee and sourdough toast and looking through the previous years' fliers that Iris had made for the Christmas festival at the ranch. She kept listening for signs that Colt and Ryder were awake, but all was silent upstairs. She had no doubt the baby would be up for the morning any minute. Along with his too-attractive father.

She was 99 percent sure she'd done the right thing last night—not rushing to help. Not really helping at all except to make a suggestion, which Colt had taken. And which had worked. What he needed was the time and space to discover that he could take care of his own baby just fine. He wasn't CEO here. He wasn't CEO of Ryder. He was just Daddy.

She tilted her head up toward the stairs when she thought she heard some movement. But then there was silence again. Ava was used to quiet, too used to it, so she was hoping the big and small Dawsons would wake up soon and fill her house with noise.

She sipped her coffee and spread out the two fliers. Iris, the least social person on earth, given how she lived, seemed to have put on the festival the past two years only to raise revenue out of pure desperation. She'd charged a five-dollar entry fee, which had included meeting and petting the six alpacas, learning about the furry creatures, including all about shearing and fiber-making, and a craft for kids to make an ornament in the shape of an alpaca. There were also refreshments—cider, eggnog and Christmas cookies.

How on earth had Iris managed all that on her own? She must have had help. Perhaps the women from her knitting circle, Vivi and Maria. Ava made a mental note to call them and ask if they knew how the festival had been set up last year, if anything didn't work, how many people had actually come. If anyone came.

I would have come, had I been invited, she thought.

Why would her great-aunt hide out on this ranch, cutting off ties to family? Perhaps she'd ask the knitting circle members that, too. There must have been some kind of rift between Iris and a relative at some point and that had been that. Ava's mother hadn't known and apparently she'd tried a few times to reach out but she'd always been rebuffed. Just like Ava had been over the years until she'd finally given up. Maybe some people were just loners like Star. Maybe it was that simple. Or maybe something had happened.

She went over to the window and looked out. The snow had stopped overnight, and there was a good three inches on the ground. Hardly the storm that had been forecast. She went back to the table and attached the fliers to the refrigerator with magnets. She'd work on that after her morning chores. If she wanted to host the festival here a few days before Christmas, she needed to get the new flier up and posted around town, create a close-to-free website since the old one—and there must have been one—had probably been canceled for lack of payment. She'd also make social media pages for the ranch so that news of the event could be shared easily. She'd get it done because she had to.

A door opened upstairs. Footsteps. Ava felt her heartbeat quicken at the anticipation of seeing both Colt and Ryder. She hoped he'd still be in the University of Wyoming T-shirt he'd worn last night and the dark blue sweats, his feet bare. She'd thought seeing Colt Dawson look like a cowboy was something until she'd seen him all mussed and bedtime casual. Sexy didn't begin to cover it.

He came downstairs with Ryder in his arms. In the T-shirt and sweats. Barefoot. Taking up her entire kitchen doorway with how male he was, how good-looking.

His shirt was a little wet as if Ryder drooled all over him. Or maybe Colt was still not quite a champ at diaper changing.

"I need to be honest with you about something," he said, looking a bit sheepish.

"Okay," she prompted, bracing herself.

"I went to change Ryder's diaper and managed to make a rookie move. Mind watching him while I take a shower and bury this shirt?"

She laughed. "Go ahead. Happens to everyone, by the way."

"It's happened to me a *few* times—and until I arrived here, I rarely changed his diapers, so a few is *a lot*. Never seems to happen to Haley and she doesn't even have a baby." He shook his head with a rueful smile. "Back in a flash."

"Take your time," she said. "I'm happy to hang out with this little dude. Oh, and toss the shirt in the hallway bathroom hamper."

The smile he gave her could melt the snow

outside. She took Ryder, who smelled like baby wipes and cornstarch, and glanced over at Colt taking the stairs two at a time.

"Morning, sweetness," she said. She took the last bite of her toast and then brought Ryder over to the window overlooking the barn. "We're gonna go see the alpacas very soon."

Ryder was staring up at her, his blue eyes so focused on her face that for a crazy moment she felt like Jocelyn was telling her it was okay. Not that she hadn't made the promise, but that Ava had told Colt what he wanted to know. *I'm gone anyway*, she could hear Jocelyn say with a whip of her long dark hair past each shoulder.

She was probably rationalizing. But the thought made her feel better anyway. She stood there, the bright morning sunshine like a balm through the glass, swaying a bit for Ryder.

"I'm a terrible singer but do you want to hear a Christmas song?" He still stared up at her. Expressionless the way babies looked sometimes. "How about 'Rudolph the Red-Nosed Reindeer'? Your daddy read you a book about a reindeer who didn't like the snow, remember? Maybe he'll finish reading it to you tonight." She sang the song, the smile bursting out on Ryder's face making her laugh.

I'll never have one of you, she thought, her

heart clenching. *Just my rotten luck. But I can think more about adoption once I get this ranch up and going again. A little boy like you? A girl?*

She forced her attention on the majestic evergreen beside the barn, perfect for the main Christmas tree that she would decorate with yards of white lights for the festival.

"So, Ryder," she said, "think I can plan and put on a Christmas festival in less than three weeks and that people will actually come and know this place is back in biz?" She had an idea about that. With some twinkling lights, garland and beautiful wreaths on the barn and the front door of the house, the ranch would be dressed up for the holiday.

But she'd need help. A team of elves. *Or one big strong cowboy like the man currently in my shower and—*

She gasped as an idea came to her. She stared at Ryder, then out at the snow-covered fields and barn, the ranch looking Christmasy just thanks to Mother Nature.

Hmm… She bit her lip, thinking it over, half scared, half elated.

I have one hell of an idea, Ryder, she told the baby silently. *I have no idea if your father will go for it, though. It involves him. And you. And this place. My entire future.*

"Christmas festival? Oh, and by the way, I love that you talk to Ryder. I do that all the time, too."

Ava turned and there was Colt, his hair damp. He wore a green Henley shirt and dark jeans and socks. Thank *God* she hadn't said any of that last part out loud.

She explained about finding the fliers for the past two years, how her usually people-shy great-aunt put on the festival to raise money, probably as some kind of last-ditch effort. "Follow me for coffee and I'll show you the fliers."

Keeping hold of Ryder, she went into the kitchen so aware of Colt right behind her. She could smell his shampoo—her shampoo. She put Ryder in the baby swing on the table and buckled him up, then poured two more mugs of coffee as Colt pulled the fliers off the refrigerator.

"Nice idea," he said, looking them over. "My cousins' dude ranch does this every Christmas, a tradition started by their grandparents over fifty years ago. People come from all over. The first Christmas, the one-day festival attracted so many people to see the petting zoo and the horses and crafts tables and hot cocoa in the lodge that the ranch ended up booked through the following summer. My cousins had to build new groupings of guest cabins."

She brightened. "That's heartening. People do like Christmas cheer. And what's more cheerful than alpacas wearing Santa hats—just for a photo opp, not to annoy them any longer than I'd have to."

She watched him add cream and sugar to his coffee. *Just tell him your grand idea*, she thought. *He's too kind to laugh at you. He'll just turn you down gently if it's a no.*

He leaned against the counter, all six-three of him, sipping his coffee and reading through the flier description from two years ago. "This sounds great. It'll take some work to get the ranch ready for visitors, though. And to set up the festival."

There was her in. *Out with it, Ava Guthrie. Just ask.*

"I'll make you a deal, Colt."

He tilted his head. "I'm usually the deal maker. I'm listening."

Okay, here goes everything. "Stay here at the ranch till Christmas," she said. "Fix what needs fixing. Teach me what you know about being a rancher. Help me get this place ready for the one-day festival. And I'll teach you about babies and give you the time and space you need to learn how to be the father you *want* to be."

He was clearly listening—intently—but he hadn't said a word, his expression hadn't changed, and she couldn't tell what he was thinking. He put his mug on the counter, then returned the fliers to the refrigerator.

Please say yes.

"We can switch off with the work that needs doing so you'll get lots of time with Ryder," she added. "If Christmas comes and goes and your heart is calling you back to the office and seventy hours a week, so be it. You'll hire a great nanny or keep Ryder at your cousins' day care. But maybe you'll find you're happiest on a ranch. By the time you leave here, you'll be a champion dad *and* you'll know what comes next for you, whether that's the office or buying your own ranch."

The slightest shift in his eyes let her know he wasn't completely opposed. But not hating the idea and doing it were two very different things. He was planning on going back to work on Wednesday.

"I don't know, Ava. I need to think about it."

Okay. That wasn't a no.

She nodded. "Of course. I'd better get to the

barn and take care of the alpacas. I'm running a bit behind. So help yourself to breakfast. There are bagels and toast and eggs, bacon. Just hunt through the fridge." She sucked in a breath and turned to Ryder. "See you later, lil guy." Then she practically ran out of the kitchen and to the front door, getting into her down jacket and hat and stuffing her pockets with her gloves.

He's not going to say yes, she thought, her stomach churning.

Okay, take a step back yourself, she told herself. *He's not your knight in shining armor, not your Prince Charming. You weren't counting on him two days ago when you never expected to see him again and you shouldn't count on him now. You can only count on yourself.*

She had a lot of Christmas wishes. And now one of them was that yes from Colt.

Not quite an hour later, while Ryder sat in his stroller, batting at the sturdy mobile that hung down and played lullabies, Colt worked on the barn door that wasn't hanging properly, Ava's surprise deal front and center in his mind.

He could see her right now through the open barn windows. She was in the pasture with the alpacas. When he'd come out with the stroller, fortified by a mug of coffee and a banana, a granola bar from her stash in his coat pocket, he'd been surprised to see she'd already shoveled a path to the barn, which he would have done. He'd waved to her and she waved back, and for a moment, he just watched her, slipping each big furry animal a treat of some kind, patting them. Star, the loner, was near the edge of the pasture, just standing there looking funny and cute. The white ones were lying down like Ava had said they sometimes did, sunbathing in the bright winter sunshine. It was cold but there was no wind and the sun made it feel almost spring-like.

In the barn he'd discovered she'd cleaned the big pen and laid out fresh straw. She was fast and solid and worked the way he did when he'd been a cowboy. She'd gotten the work done—and well. It was clearly how she'd managed as a total rookie out here on her own the past four months.

He'd found the tools he needed in the barn shed and got to work, too. When Ryder let out a cry, he forced himself to give him a minute instead of running over. He watched his son—*his* son, he repeated in his head—shift a bit, then bat at the little orange monkey and let out a big laugh. So sometimes he had to step back, like now, and sometimes he had step in, like last night. Maybe one of these days that would become less foggy.

He couldn't take Ava's deal, could he? Stay here through Christmas? He did want to help her. And yeah, she needed help, competent as she was. Especially if she was going to put on that holiday festival. This ranch wasn't a one-woman operation even if she'd done it for four months. She *was* running herself ragged.

And what was he doing? Barging into her room with a shrieking baby at two in the morning like he wasn't the parent. The sole parent.

Buck the hell up, he told himself. No more of that.

Which made her offer so damned tempting. So completely...right.

Time away from the all-consuming office. Time to learn to be the father he wanted to be. Time on a ranch, even one without cattle and horses or even sheep. He *needed* the deal.

But what might clinch it was the bitterness he'd heard in his voice when he called his sister a little while ago to tell her he'd be here for a while, maybe a couple of days, maybe longer, he'd let her know.

Wait, you're staying at Ava's alpaca ranch for a few days? Haley had said, surprise in her voice.

She knows everything...about Ryder, he'd explained. *I don't have to talk about it, but if I want to, she has the answer. If I come home, if I go back to work, my head will explode with it. So I'm here for at least another couple days.*

Sounds like it's exactly where you need to be, Colt.

He knew only that he didn't want to leave yet. No way was he walking back into his regular world with that damned letter in his head. He'd been lied to about something so fundamental. Yes, he was bitter.

He paused with the power drill in his hand, looking over at Ryder, now banging on the tray of his stroller, big happy smile.

You are my son, no matter what, he said silently for the hundredth time. No matter what.

But the lie? The sickening betrayal? That rubbed raw.

And out here on this ranch—this needy alpaca ranch—it was just him, Ryder and the woman who, as he'd told Haley, knew, understood. He could stand silently beside her and feel the weight of her understanding. That was what he needed. He could just be out here, like his cousin Ford had suggested almost a month ago. Now he had more reason to *just be*. If he could.

Which was where the deal came in. In his world, you made a deal and you signed on it. He'd be staying till Christmas. Two and a half weeks away. Just the right amount of time, maybe. To be. To let some things sit and work their way through his veins.

He'd have to call his co-CEO and his staff. Haley would tell their cousins something about where he'd gone that would be just right; that was Haley's gift.

When Ava came in the side door from the pasture, her cheeks slightly reddened from the cold, her pale pink hat pulled low over her ears, he had his answer. Her answer.

Their answer.

"You've got a deal, Ava Guthrie," he said.

The relief that fell over her expression, that relaxed her shoulders, that had her bending down to exhale before briefly closing her eyes, made him realize how badly she needed this. For her own reasons, of course.

"Good thing you brought your cowboy hat, then," she said, coming over to him and extending her hand.

He took her hand and shook it, then grasped it with both of his. She couldn't have said something more fitting, more right, and he wanted to

just pull her to him and hold her for even just fifteen seconds. For the first time since he found
that letter in the desk, he felt his feet were on
solid ground.

Chapter Seven

Ava sat at the scarred old desk in her aunt Iris's office, a small room on the first floor that was jam-packed with file cabinets. She'd gone poking through the desk and closet and a few of the files over the months, but hadn't found what she'd been looking for: anything personal. Today, fortified by Colt's yes about staying through Christmas and helping each other out, she was hoping to come across information about the previous two years' festivals. But Iris's piles and files, overflowing out of the cabinets into neat but scary stacks on the floor, were a mishmash of thirty years.

She swiveled in the padded wood chair, a true joy bubbling up inside her again. To know she had Colt's help. That she could help him. That she could spend this precious time with the baby who meant so much to her. Talk about a Christmas gift. After they'd shaken on their deal, Colt had said he'd better finish up the barn door be-

fore it was time to change Ryder and work on
tummy time, which made her smile, and she'd
come inside the house to give Colt some space
with their arrangement.

He was already seeing that he could work at
the ranch and care for Ryder—both to a point,
of course—at the same time. He'd factored in
the need to change Ryder and do some develop-
mental tummy work instead of either letting the
diaper go a little too long or asking Ava to do it.
He'd have his time with Ryder and then get back
to work on the ranch. On only his and Ryder's
schedule. And last night, of course, had to have
done wonders to make him see what he could do
if he just allowed himself.

She pulled out her phone and looked through
her contacts for Vivi's or Maria's numbers. She
found both, which they'd entered into her phone
after the funeral. She'd do a group text.

Hi, Vivi and Maria. Any chance we could meet to
talk about the Christmas festival Iris put on the
last two years? I'd like to continue the tradition.

Viva responded immediately with two emojis—
a ball of yarn and a coffee cup—and: How about
tomorrow at 1pm. I'll bring a great quiche. Maria

and I were going to have lunch so we'll bring the lunch to you!

Ava sent back an alpaca emoji and a see you then.

Everything was looking up, she thought. *I'm going to get to know you through your beloved ranch, Aunt Iris. Forgive me for digging around in your life. It would mean so much to me to understand you so that I'm on more solid ground here. I want to do right by you.*

So far, she'd done just fine with the alpacas, getting by, sure, but fine. And now that she had great help in the six-foot-three, muscular form of Colt Dawson, she could achieve her big goals for the ranch. And the festival was a surefire way to start.

Iris had an ancient desktop computer that Ava had moved to a closet, her own laptop front and center of the desk. She opened up the template app and with the two previous fliers beside her, she decided to go for what Iris knew worked and a bit more contemporary approach. She'd taken at least a hundred photos of the alpacas over the past four months so there were some great ones to choose from. Her favorite was one in which all six were lined up horizontally at the pasture fence and looking like they were smiling. Ava put that photo across the top along with a shot of the big, pretty sign at the entrance to the ranch. *Prairie Hills Alpaca Ranch* and a little alpaca were carved into the wood. Iris must have had the sign special made in financially better times. After she met with Vivi and Maria tomorrow, she'd write up the description of the festival's events and get the flier posted around town and online by Wednesday.

This is going to happen, she thought. *Iris, you might not have let me know you, but I'm going to do you and the alpacas proud. Just when I needed somewhere to go, you gave me this haven, this special farm that I've come to care deeply about.*

She rested a foot on one of the milk crates under the desk. They were full of old papers and files that she'd poked through, but they were mostly the last five years of ranch business. Maybe Colt could go through the past year's books, see what it might tell him about what she could do for the future.

She got up and went to the closet. There was just one piece of clothing on the top shelf, an old heather-gray cardigan sweater that Iris has been wearing when she'd been rushed to the hospital. When Ava arrived, her great-aunt had asked to find out what happened to her cardigan because she wanted to wear it, it was her favorite. Ava had asked a nurse, and when she'd come for visiting hours that evening, Iris had been wearing the sweater. The morning she'd lost Iris, a nurse had mentioned to Ava that she'd packed it into a bag with the few other items Iris had with her. She'd looked in the bag; there was the thick gray sweater and a cross-body fabric bag with an empty baggie in it; Ava figured she'd used it to hold treats for the alpacas. She'd put the folded sweater and fabric bag on the closet shelf in the office as a tribute to the businesswoman, the alpaca devotee, who'd run the ranch.

Ava reached up for the sweater and put it on, wondering if it would give her strength. She put her hands in the long front pockets—there was something inside. She pulled it out and gasped.

A photograph. A young couple, maybe late twenties, by a lake, smiling, the guy's arm slung around her shoulder.

Ava held the photo closer. Was that Iris? She was pretty sure it was. Iris was tall and thin and though her hair had been a silver-white in the hospital, she'd mentioned to Ava that she'd once had hair the same color as Ava's. A light blond. Just like the woman in the photo. She turned it over, hoping there would be names. There were. *Iris and Jack. Hopper's Lake. August.*

Jack. Who was Jack? Iris had never gotten married and Ava couldn't remember ever hearing about a man in her life. But clearly there had been.

What was the story with Iris and Jack? Ava was dying to know. If the photo was in the pocket of her favorite sweater, the one she'd been wearing when she'd been rushed to the hospital… Had she always kept it there? Had she known she was getting sick and weak and went looking for the old photo and put it in her pocket as a cherished memory? There were so many possibilities. She sat down at the desk and studied the picture. Jack was handsome, tall and lanky, with a warm smile and dark eyes, light brown thick hair. He wore a T-shirt and shorts, same as Iris.

"Ava?"

Colt. She put the photo in the desk drawer for safekeeping.

"Coming," she called out, heading to find him.

He stood by the front door, taking off his coat, then unbuckling Ryder and getting him out of his fleece bunting.

For a moment she imagined kissing him hello and taking the baby to give him a nuzzle.

As though Colt were hers. As though Ryder were hers. Her guys, home from their work in the barn.

"Just a couple things left to take care of in the barn," he said, his blue eyes holding that same sparkle as when he'd come in last time from cowboy work. "I'll play with Ryder upstairs for a while and then once he's down for his nap, I thought we could have a meeting."

"A meeting?" she asked.

"About how our deal is going to work. The moving parts."

Oh good grief. "Colt, you're a cowboy here. A dad. Not CEO. We don't take meetings and put pins in ideas or use the word *wheelhouse*. Wheelbarrow, maybe."

He tilted his head as if he had no idea what she was talking about, then he grinned. "Did I say *meeting*? I meant sit and talk. Which is really the same thing."

She laughed. "Just trying to get you into the spirit of the ranch. We're casual around here."

"Speaking of spirit," he said, "think your aunt has Christmas decorations somewhere? Attic? Basement? I can get started stringing lights outside for the festival after I finish up in the barn later. And a wreath for the front door and the barn would be great. Garland around the outer gates where the alpacas can't mistake it for interesting-colored straw."

She grimaced. "I'm not sure I would have thought about that—the alpacas eating it. I might have wrapped it right around the fencing if you hadn't said that." Her stomach twisted at the thought of any of the alpacas getting injured or sick because of her. So far, they were okay. But that really was because she'd had the vet out here so often those first two months.

"Hey, don't be so hard on yourself. You've been at this for four months. Alone. Cut yourself a very big break."

She appreciated that. Hadn't she been saying the same to him about fatherhood?

"I just realized we've both been at these new lives for exactly the same amount of time. Four months. Alpaca rancher for me. Fatherhood for you."

"I'm not used to being new at anything," he said.

"Should I not mention that every stage, every age, brings something new to parenthood?"

He smiled. "Definitely don't mention that. I'm already scared of teething. I think that's coming soon. But don't worry, that's a couple months away at least, so we'll be long gone by then. No screaming baby to wake you up."

She almost gasped. *Long gone by then.*

Of course he would be. He would take Ryder and leave right after Christmas. Their deal kept him here that long.

She'd better be very careful of not falling for the two Dawsons, one big, one little.

Colt had spent a little over an hour playing with Ryder in their room, and was now back in the barn, the baby in his stroller, batting away at his stuffed animal and little fabric book with chewable edges.

"See these hay bales?" Colt asked Ryder, pointing to the opposite corner where the bales were lying haphazardly. "I'm going to make four piles of four so Ava can easily get to them, but stack them neatly so they're out of the way."

Her aunt had likely been unable to move them herself and same for Ava. He glanced around. One stall, likely used for when an alpaca needed to be isolated while recuperating from an injury or illness, had a busted gate, so he'd take care of that next.

"Alpacas eat grass and hay," he told Ryder. "Same as horses, but did you know there are different types of hay, depending on how its cut? Horses and alpacas don't eat the same kind." While he'd been unable to sleep last night, he'd done a little reading up on alpacas, no idea then that he'd be sticking around for a couple of weeks. Now he was glad he'd done some research.

While Colt worked, he kept up a running commentary to Ryder of what he was doing. He froze, hay bale in his arms, when he realized his own father had done the same. Making Colt sit on his leather Chesterfield in his home office while he bored him to death about the projections for the coming quarter. Who was up for a department directorship this year. Which companies Godfrey and Dawson were thinking of buying and which they were selling.

Colt had squirmed, his mind on horses, his dad yelling at him to pay attention. Dragging him into the Godfrey and Dawson office every few months to show him the ropes, making him shadow this VP or that. Colt had dreaded those times, but now that he was talking nonstop to Ryder about ranch work, which of course he assumed Ryder found interesting, he realized his father had been *sharing*. Forcing, yeah. But sharing. And sharing what was very important to him. He'd never thought of it that way before. Of course, then,

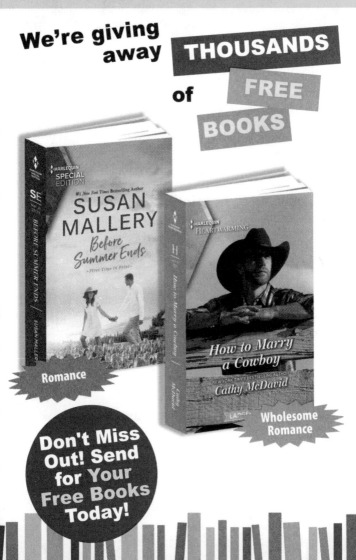

Get up to 4
FREE FABULOUS BOOKS
You Love!

To thank you for being a loyal reader we'd like to send you up to 4 FREE BOOKS, absolutely free.

Just write "YES" on the Loyal Reader Voucher and we'll send you up to 4 Free Books and Free Mystery Gifts, altogether worth over $20, as a way of saying thank you for being a loyal reader.

Try **Harlequin® Special Edition** books featuring comfort and strength in the support of loved ones and enjoying the journey no matter what life throws your way.

Try **Harlequin® Heartwarming™ Larger-Print** books featuring uplifting stories where the bonds of friendship, family and community unite.

Or **TRY BOTH!**

We are so glad you love the books as much as we do and can't wait to send you great new books.

So don't miss out, return your Loyal Reader Voucher Today!

Pam Powers

LOYAL READER
FREE BOOKS VOUCHER

Colt hadn't been in his dad's shoes in that regard. Now he was. And as Ryder grew up, whatever interested him, whatever was his great passion, Colt would encourage it.

He'd definitely take this barn that smelled of hay and livestock over a boardroom any day. He glanced out the window at the cloudless blue sky and could see trees, land and mountains stretching in the distance, the alpacas pushing their noses in the snow. At Godfrey and Dawson, he'd be fueled by coffee and adrenaline for the merger, the deal, his cell phone in his hand at all times, admins and VPs knocking on his door, chasing him down the hall with questions or to sign something on the way to another meeting. Here, he was looking at his son in a silent barn.

"This is a good place, Ryder. Needs work, but it'll get there."

Ryder batted his fabric book against his stroller tray with a giggle.

"I knew you agreed," Colt said, grinning. "Okay, one last bale to go."

Hay all stacked, he got to work on the broken stall gate. Once that was finished, he wheeled Ryder back to the house and found Ava in the living room, working on her laptop.

"Good or bad time to watch Ryder for about

twenty minutes?" he asked. "I'd like to see how the garland looks wrapped around the fence posts and the tree by the entrance to the ranch, too."

Her face lit up. "Very good time. And Colt, thanks for all you're doing. You're like three cowboys in one."

"More like an eighth of a cowboy," he said. "It's been a long time since I've done the kind of work I did this morning. But it comes back fast."

"A true love for something always does," she said.

He supposed so. He tipped his hat at her, told Ryder to be a good boy, grabbed the box she'd brought up from the basement earlier and headed back out. When he was done decorating, the alpacas watching him sometimes but ignoring him for the most part, he stepped back to see how it looked.

Festive.

Between the red garland and the snow-covered pastures, the cute alpacas, the ranch suddenly looked Christmasy. Add the sparkling white lights, a big wreath for the top of the barn and one for the door, and the place would be magical. He glanced toward the front window and there was Ava holding Ryder. She waved at him, and he could just make out her smile.

He wished they were out here beside him. Something about Ava Guthrie, maybe just everything he'd put in words to his sister, made him feel shored up somehow. He waved back, unable to look away. This woman. His son.

He was three hours into the deal with Ava and it felt good and right. But this…attraction he felt for her, the draw—he wasn't going to act on that. As good as Ava felt in his arms the few times he'd held her, she didn't belong there. No one did.

It was him and Ryder now, and that was the way he wanted it. Ryder was completely innocent in everything that had driven him out to this ranch. But people, the people closest to you, like your wife, could lie right in your face without blinking an eye. He couldn't imagine ever trusting another woman.

He went back inside and shrugged out of his coat and took off his hat. Ava and Ryder were now in the kitchen, Ryder in his swing on the table, a speaker on the counter softly playing "Deck the Halls." Ava was making sandwiches, and he realized he was starving.

"Ham and Swiss on rye?" she asked. "I could make paninis, if you want."

"The sandwich is just fine," he said. "And thank you."

She brought over their plates and two bottles of water and sat down across from him. "The fence looks so festive," she said. "What a difference."

He nodded and took a bite of his sandwich. "And it's just some garland. Imagine once the lights are up. This place will look like a Christmas wonderland. You know, I just realized you don't have a tree yet."

His cousins had set up a huge tree in the family room of his house, and his sister had gone to town trimming it, but he hadn't exactly felt festive the past month and barely looked at it. He had no doubt it was the same for her. This had been a time of loss for both of them.

"I wasn't planning on getting one," she said. "I figured it would make me feel sad, celebrating all alone out at the ranch. My parents gone too young. And this year, my great-aunt gone before I even know her. My best friend after the worst argument I've ever had. I love Christmas, but this is a weird one."

"Yeah, it is. And you're not alone. I'm here. Ryder's here. And like you said, you love Christmas. That house needs some serious cheering up. I want to get you a tree as a gift from me to you for our good deal."

"It *is* a good deal," she'd said. "Okay. A tree. I

have a box of ornaments that I brought over in the move to the ranch."

He pulled out his phone, did some googling and found a Christmas tree farm that also sold wreaths just ten minutes from here. He held up the site. "Let's go after Ryder's nap. While he's asleep, we can have that meeting—I mean, *talk*—about our arrangement. Set the agenda. The… What would you call it in noncorporate speak?"

She laughed. "Maybe it is a little nice having a CEO around here," she said, taking a bite of her sandwich. "You get things done, Colt Dawson."

He reached over and touched her hand and she squeezed it. Again he was struck by how close he felt to her. But he had to remember he was leaving in two and a half weeks, going back to Bear Ridge, back to his life. There was a 5 percent chance, probably less, that he'd ever leave Godfrey and Dawson. But he'd have this break, this Christmas with his son, on this alpaca ranch.

With a woman who made him think of reaching for the stars, even if he wouldn't.

Chapter Eight

A half hour later, Ava sat on one end of the sofa, Colt on the other, both with pads and pens on their laps. Discussion time.

Colt was looking around the room. "Plush tan sofas, a kilim rug, floor pillows. Abstract art on the walls. I'm surprised the living room doesn't match the paint upstairs and the floral wallpaper in the bathrooms."

"I brought my furniture from my condo," she said. "When I got here, everything was so unfamiliar that I knew I had to bring my own things to feel connected, more comfortable. So I donated Iris's furniture and sent a moving truck for my own. It helped. I did keep a lot of Iris's things, though."

His gaze went to a framed photograph of Iris with two of the alpacas—Lorelai and Rory—on the mantel. "So she lived here alone? She never married, never had kids?"

"Nope. Apparently, she bought this place when

she was twenty-nine. I don't know much about the history, other than she got the land for a song and fixed up the run-down house and barn. But she stayed here alone, building her ranch, her industry with yarns and fleece-stuffed duvets and pillows. She had two friends that I know of, the women from her knitting circle. They're coming tomorrow afternoon to tell me how the festival worked last year."

"One o'clock, right? I'll keep Ryder occupied so you three can talk."

"Sounds good," she said.

"That and this entire morning has been a great example of how our arrangement can work," he said. "When I had to do something and I couldn't keep an eye on Ryder or if he'd be freezing in no time, I asked you if you were free to watch him. Is that too up in the air for you, though? He's on a schedule but he's portable. Your schedule might not be as flexible."

"I can always spread straw or clean out the pens earlier or later, depending on when you need me to hang with Ryder. I think it's working great, too."

"Good. Then we're done. Quickest not-a-meeting ever."

But don't get up. Don't leave. Don't go upstairs. Just stay.

He was so close. Just a few feet away, tall and muscular all over her couch. *Maybe I'm back*, she thought. After two years of staying single, of being afraid to even date because of how her ex-fiancé left her because she couldn't have children of her own, all her nerve endings were tingling. She wanted to kiss Colt Dawson.

Maybe because she knew this was a finite thing. That he was leaving in under three weeks. But if the way she already felt about him, the pull to him, the anticipation of seeing him, talking to him, being near him was any indication, she was in real danger of falling in love with him.

So back off, she ordered herself. *Just do nothing.*

Get back to the ranch. "Vivi and Maria will be able to give us the lowdown on the festival. How it went, how the prep was. I got the feeling from meeting them at the funeral and a couple times since that they really cared about Iris and miss her. I'm glad they're coming. These past four months I've been too busy to do anything other than take care of the ranch and fall into bed."

"I'm glad I'm here for you, Ava. I'm glad we're here for each other."

"Me, too," she said.

They were looking at each other—a little too

long, and suddenly he got up and walked around the room, looking at the bookshelf.

Where there were two photos of her and Jocelyn. One from high school and one from a few years ago, when they treated each other to a spa day since their birthdays were the same month. Facials. Massages. Mani-pedis. In that photo they were lounging on the deck, each holding up a frozen margarita. Ava didn't spend a lot of time in the living room; she was mostly in the kitchen at the table or her bedroom or the barn, so she'd set out the photos because she wanted them in the house but just not where she would see them readily.

"It's awful being mad at someone who's gone," he said. "The mother of your child."

"I think time will help with that. Right now, it's very raw."

He picked up the photo of them with the drinks. "I wonder why it was so important to her that I not know that Ryder isn't mine. Our marriage was so bad toward the end it's a wonder she didn't throw it in my face. She could have used it against me quite a few times."

Ava knew a little too much about their marriage, how strained things were between them. "Like I said yesterday, Jocelyn loved you, Colt. Yes, she did what she did. And the two of you may not have been a match in many ways, but she loved you."

"Loved me or the lifestyle I provided her with?" he asked, bitterness lacing his voice.

"She loved you. I know she did. You know she did. But she was Jocelyn and we both know *that*."

He put down the photo and came back to the sofa and sat down, letting his head drop back on the cushion. "I don't know what the hell I'd do if I didn't have you to talk to, Ava."

"That goes double for me."

He turned to face her and reached out a hand to her face. The connection felt so good. So, so good. She closed her eyes for a second, her heart starting to beat faster, faster, faster. And she felt him move closer.

He was inches away. His blue eyes on her. Intently. And then he kissed her. Softy at first, and then he moved in, one hand in her hair, the other around her back.

Then he pulled away. "I definitely shouldn't have done that."

"But I'm glad you did," she dared say.

He reached for her hand again and held it for a second. "Complicated," he finally said.

"Very, very complicated," she agreed with a shaky nod. For a lot of reasons. She wasn't sure if the fact that he was here temporarily, just for a couple of more weeks, made it worse or not.

He *was* like a Christmas gift. She'd have to give him back, but maybe she could let herself have this for a couple of weeks. They would help each other in more ways than one.

"Maybe we should do what feels right," she said. "Complicated or not. And not overthink it. You're leaving, so we know up front no attachments allowed."

You're leaving and taking Ryder with you, she amended silently. She was already attached to both of them after such a short time. Two weeks from now? Working together? Living in the same house? At Christmas?

She bit her lip and turned away. "Forget what I said a minute ago. We don't need complicated on top of complicated."

He leaned his head back again and she could barely drag her eyes off his frame.

"Why didn't you make her that promise?" he asked suddenly, turning his head to look at her.

"Just felt wrong," she managed to say, her voice breaking. "She accused me of being jealous that she was doing something about the fact that she couldn't get pregnant."

He sat up and stared at her. "What do you mean?"

"I can't have children. I've known since I was in my early twenties. I was engaged a couple years ago, you probably remember that."

"I remember going to the engagement party," he said. "And that the four of us went out to dinner a few times."

"Two days before the wedding he told me he couldn't marry a woman who couldn't have children."

He winced. "I'm so sorry. That shouldn't matter. You could adopt."

"He was focused on 'bloodlines' apparently." She gave a little shrug, trying not to remember the breakup. He'd even asked for the ring back. Sliding it off her finger made her feel like she was being returned for being defective. "It's probably the main reason Jocelyn didn't want you to know about Ryder—she was afraid that with your dad and grandfather being so invested in bloodlines and the family name, that you'd care, too."

He shook his head. "I wish she'd known me better than that. But that speaks to what our marriage was like."

"And what my marriage would have been like," she said. "We weren't meant to be but it took me a while to see it."

He moved closer and pulled her into his arms

and just held her. "Sorry, Ava. You've been through a lot."

"Hey, I've got the alpacas. And this place. A piece of my aunt who I never got to know. A big piece. I'll be okay. One of these days."

The hand was back on her face. And then his lips were back on hers.

Never stop kissing me, she thought.

"This is dangerous," he said. "I think when Ryder wakes up we should go get that Christmas tree and keep ourselves very busy decorating it."

"Good idea," she agreed, wishing he was still kissing her.

But she scooted over a bit, and his arms came from around her. She missed the comfort and warmth immediately.

Colt pulled into a spot in the gravel driveway of the Johannsen Family Christmas Tree Farm, Ava beside him, Ryder in his rear-facing car seat in the back. Once again, she was way too close. He was too aware of her, his attraction to her, his *need* for her.

That kiss. That second kiss. Holding her. Wanting so much more. They'd gotten lucky—Ryder had started fussing upstairs, and it gave them the excuse to get up that minute. She'd disappeared into her office, and he'd gone to the nursery to get Ryder.

When Colt had picked him up, cuddling him against his chest, the fussing stopped. "I've got you, little guy," he'd said, Ryder's huge blue eyes on him. Trusting him to be there, to take care of him.

Colt had known right then and there that he had to keep his hands, his lips off Ava Guthrie. His whole point of being here was to connect with his son. To learn to be a father. To get back his equilibrium after that damned letter.

He was here to breathe and settle. Not get involved with a woman who for twenty different reasons was off-limits.

Focus your non-Ryder attention on helping her get the ranch up and running, he'd told himself. *With the Christmas festival. Do what you're here for.*

"That's some tree," Ava said, nodding at the big spruce an employee was helping tie down to the top of the truck beside them.

"Every Christmas tree should be 'some tree,'" he said. "Spectacular to you. You'll know the one when you see it. And while we're here," he added, getting out the list he'd made earlier, "let's get a wreath for the door and a huge one for the outside of the barn, maybe one with lights. We'll have the ranch decorated for the festival early on and it'll help generate good ideas every time we're outside. Your aunt had plenty of garland and yards and yards of lights, so we're set there."

There you go, he thought. *Keep your head in Christmas, in helping Ava with the festival.*

She bit her lip, then turned to him. "Colt, thing is, I'll have to pay you back sometime in the future when the ranch starts making money again. Iris's accounts dried up long ago. And I had some savings, but it's getting depleted, too, on just the most basic running of the ranch. I set a budget for what I need for the festival so I can cover that."

"Ava, I've got it. No worries. I want you to get everything that you want for the festival. If people are going to come later in the spring and summer for children's camps and workshops, they'll want to see a ranch in excellent working order, a ranch that can put on a really special Christmas fair."

"That's exactly what I was thinking. I'll keep a list of what I owe you. I know the ranch will come back," she said. "I promised Iris once she was gone that I'd take care of her alpacas and the farm, and I intend to."

Something else they had in common. One

deathbed promise, one sent after, heavenward. But both had turned both their lives upside down, taken them down unexpected roads. Except Ava seemed to love where her new life had led. "I have no doubt you will," he said. "But Christmas is on me, including the festival. If you don't let me do it for you, let me do it for Ryder. This is his first Christmas."

She brightened. "Okay, when you put it that way. And thank you. I have my pride, Colt, but I don't turn down help when I need it."

He squeezed her hand and they got out of the car. He could tell she was uncomfortable about letting him pay. But now that he knew how bad things were at the ranch, he was about to make life there a lot more comfortable. He wouldn't tell her. He'd just take care of what needed attention, order what was required, make sure she was set up for the new year and ongoing, when he'd be gone.

Gone.

The thought of leaving her behind left a hollowness in his chest. He cared about her, clearly. They needed each other right now and it was probably hard to think about leaving when he'd just gotten here, when they were at the start of their deal.

With Ryder in a carrier strapped to his chest, they went up and down the rows of the tree farm, narrowly avoiding a snowball thrown their way by two kids chasing each other. "Jingle Bells" was playing on a speaker.

"That's the one," she said. "Not too big, not too small. Just right. It's a beauty."

It was. The tree was a seven-foot-tall Fraser fir, a good choice with its stiff branches that would hold lots of ornaments.

"It smells heavenly. Like Christmas," she said. "Gee, I wonder why. It's a Christmas tree." She laughed, and it felt good to see her happy, not worried or strained as she'd been in the car about finances. Or…unsure, like back at the house, when they'd been all over each other. For a start, anyway. A start that he'd see didn't go on.

"What do you think, Ryder?" he asked. "A beaut, am I right?"

Ryder tried to bat at the branches, which told them he agreed.

"This is going to be a great Christmas, Ava," Colt said. He knew this because he was going to make sure of it. Even the alpacas would have an amazing Christmas.

It would be his gift to her, then he could go back home and figure out what he was going to do. Likely buy a ranch house on decent acreage not too far from the center of Bear Ridge and keep a couple of horses, rent out the big house and turn it over to Ryder when he was an adult as the home where he'd lived with both his parents. He wouldn't sell it out from under his son or take it away. It was part of Ryder's legacy. Just like the truth was. Colt would go back to Godfrey and Dawson and work hard on delegating—just like here he was working on fatherhood—so that his hours would be more manageable now that he was a single parent. But he couldn't just walk away from his responsibilities.

Once they had the tree's tag to give a staffer to lug it over to the truck for them, they went over to the wreath area. Ava picked out a traditional one with a red bow for the front door and Colt insisted on the huge one for atop the outside of the barn. While at the register inside, Ryder bought three Santa hats, one in a baby size, a carton of eggnog, which it turned out Ava liked, too, and a tin of their homemade Christmas cookies. Once the big wreath and tree were strapped to the roof of the car, their bags in the trunk, they headed back home.

Home. What he'd meant was the alpaca ranch. He supposed it was home for the next two and a half weeks. He just had to remember—at the forefront of his mind—that he was leaving after Christmas—most likely on Christmas morning—and keep to his vow to make Ava off-limits.

Chapter Nine

What a difference even the bare fir made in the living room, Ava thought, staring up at it. Tall and stately with that scent of Christmas. They'd managed to lug the giant wreath over to the barn—Colt would hang it later—and the tree into the house and set it up by the three big windows.

While Colt got busy stringing the lights around it, and with Ryder—wearing his adorable Santa hat—in his swing and shaking his giraffe rattle, Ava headed upstairs to get her box of ornaments from her closet. Most of the ornaments were red, silver and gold balls, but there were many heirloom ornaments from her childhood and ones she'd bought over the past ten years. She wondered if her aunt had ever had a Christmas tree in the house. There were decorations for outside, but no ornaments for a tree. Maybe like Ava, Iris hadn't wanted to celebrate the holiday alone, the tree too much of a reminder in her own living room.

They spent the next fifteen minutes hanging all the balls, and then Ava began choosing the ornaments. Some made her smile, some made her want to cry.

"My parents gave me an ornament in my stocking every year," she said. "I have them all, even from when I was a year old." She took out a ceramic Victorian house, meant to represent the pretty house her parents had hoped to afford one day. "My parents were both hard workers, but they never did get the house of their dreams," she said, holding up the ornament. "I always thought I'd buy it for them for their retirement once I was settled in a job, but I lost them both to illness, six years apart, when I was in my late teens, early twenties."

"I'm so sorry," he said, squeezing her hand. "I know how that is. My mother was the tree trimmer. Some Christmases my father would actually be in his den for hours, yelling on the phone about a merger or acquisition that wasn't going well. The three of us—my mom and sister and I—would just sort of freeze, waiting for him to be done, but then he'd be in such a mood that dinner was pretty much ruined."

"Why would he want to miss out on the most important thing in his life?" she asked. "I don't get it. How could a merger be more important than Christmas or his family?"

"It was," he said. "And now I'm the same way." He turned away as if just realizing it was true.

"I don't believe that about you, Colt. And this is Ryder's first everything—first Christmas, and then it'll be his first birthday. You haven't had the opportunity to be like your dad."

He seemed to consider that. "Well, I'm headed there. That's how I was in my marriage."

"You were encouraged to be that way and ran with it."

He looked surprised, as if she knew too much about his marriage, and maybe she shouldn't have said it. But it was true.

"There was a time when Jocelyn and I were really something special," he said, his gaze on the tree. "We had a great time together. But I was never ready to start a family and she pulled away more and more and there came a period of time where we would actually go a day or two without having said one word to each other."

"Like I said, if my ex-fiancé hadn't practically left me at the altar, we would have been just like that." She sighed. "I was so focused on getting thrown over for something out of my control that

I never really thought about that. I guess he did me a favor."

"Love, engagement, marriage. Things start out great and end miserably. Why even bother at all?"

Because of how I feel about you, she thought. "The start is usually irresistible. Thinking about someone all the time. Anticipating seeing them. Who doesn't want love? Romance. Smiling yourself to sleep."

"When you know it's going to end in betrayal? Like mine did? Like yours? No thanks," he said, giving one of the red balls on the tree a little push.

She watched it swing, her heart sinking. Low in her chest. But instead of trying to defend love, she found herself wanting to know something personal. Very personal.

Just change the subject. Talk about favorite holiday movies. Don't go there, Ava.

"Why didn't you want children?" she blurted out anyway. "I mean even last year Jocelyn said you were still ambivalent."

"Because I'm my father's son," he said. "I was afraid I'd be just like him and I am."

"You don't have to be, Colt. You do understand that, right? You've made choices. To work sixty to seventy hours a week. To let your sister and cousins step in for you instead of doing the heavy lifting of fatherhood yourself."

Had she said that last part? She inwardly winced, wondering if she was going too far.

He was staring at her, his eyes intense. "It's not just that I made a promise to my father to take over for him. I have responsibilities, Ava. People count on me. A lot of people."

"But your promise shouldn't mean you don't have a life outside Godfrey and Dawson," she said. "When you made that promise, you didn't have a baby. You're the sole parent now. I think you've had this idea in your head for so long that you're not meant to be a dad that you've used work as your excuse not to be the dad you could be."

No, *that* was going too far. But she couldn't help herself, couldn't keep this tamped down. He was here for honesty. Not for sugarcoating or placating.

He crossed his arms over his chest. "What do you think our deal is about? Teaching me how to do that."

"So you'll go straight back to Godfrey and Dawson? Working the same sixty to seventy hours a week? Seeing your son an hour every night and on the weekends—when you're not having to slip away to take care of the details of an acquisition despite having trusted high-level staff?"

He turned away and walked to the window. "I don't know, Ava." His voice was tired, full of regret.

She'd definitely gone too far. For now, anyway.

She wished she could walk up behind him and wrap her arms around him, lean her head against his back, tell him something comforting instead of rubbing his wounds raw. She'd pushed too far. But like he said, that was what he was here for. To be the father Ryder deserved. And who was she to tell him how to live his life? He had to *want* to be more present for his son, literally and figuratively.

"I have a good idea," she said. "I'll go pour us some of that eggnog we got from the Christmas tree farm. And we'll trim the tree and listen to the Christmas songs and smile at Ryder in his baby Santa hat. Enough heavy talking for one night."

He gave her something of a smile. "All of that sounds really good, Ava."

She smiled back and went into the kitchen and poured two cups of eggnog. Another thing they had in common. They were as good as their word and had stopped talking about themselves. She hummed along to her favorite songs, added her ornaments and sipped her eggnog.

And then the tree was done, and Colt flipped the switch.

Ava gasped. "It's so beautiful I could cry. Wow," she said, staring up at it, the star he'd affixed to the top all sparkly silver.

"We make a good team." He held up his cup to clink with hers.

She clinked and knew, without a doubt, that she was falling for this man.

Trouble, she thought, trying to keep her eyes on the tree and not her cowboy. Or on the adorable baby in his Santa hat, who suddenly let out a giant yawn. Colt had fed him before they'd started trimming, and now it was time for the little guy to hit the bassinet.

"While you're getting Ryder to bed, I can make us dinner. I've got two really good-looking steaks, asparagus and potatoes. We'll eat instead of talk. We can keep it going all night."

In bed, she added silently. A thought that had come out of nowhere unless she admitted to how often she thought about kissing Colt again, being with him...

"Actually, steaks and baked potatoes are my specialty," he said. "My only specialty. I learned to grill as a cowboy, and the stovetop would work just as well."

"Well, then how about I take care of bedtime and you cook?" she asked, realizing in the same breath that she was stepping into really dangerous territory.

This was seriously homey. Decorating the tree together. Colt making them dinner. Ava putting the baby to bed.

Colt wasn't her man. And Ryder wasn't her baby.

"Deal. Second of the day," he said.

She'd have to make a third with herself. To be careful. Or she was going to break her own heart.

Over two great steaks, baked potatoes with sour cream, and garlic-butter-drizzled asparagus, Colt and Ava had kept the conversation about the alpaca ranch and not themselves. He'd asked her to tell him everything she knew about alpacas because, one, he needed as much information on them as he could soak up and, two, he assumed it would carry the entire dinner conversation. He'd been right.

Now he knew that alpacas were the smallest members of the camel family, a newborn alpaca was called a cria—Spanish for breeding—the

noises they made, which he'd heard a few times
now, were like humming, there were only two
types of alpacas, the Suri and the Huacaya, and
Ava had all Huacayas with their shorter, more
crimped fleece than the long-haired Suri. Oh, and
alpacas didn't have teeth in the top front of their
mouths, which might account for why they could
look a bit comical. He'd learned about their hab-
its and preferences and that they generally lived
for about twenty years.

Now, it was close to three in the morning, and
he was lying on his side in bed, watching Ryder
sleep in the bassinet. With his baby son right
here, right beside him, all felt right in the world.

*But your promise shouldn't mean you don't
have a life outside Godfrey and Dawson*, he heard
Ava saying. *When you made that promise, you
didn't have a baby. You're the sole parent now.
I think you've had this idea in your head for so
long that you're not meant to be a dad that you've
used work as your excuse not to be the dad you
could be.*

No mystery why he'd never felt this peace before, being inches from his child, watching his
chest rise up and down, his little lips quirk in his
sleep, a little tremor of his hand. Because he'd

never had Ryder in a bassinet next to his bed. He'd been unaware of so much.

Maybe Ava was right about using work as an excuse to be absent. His work was his responsibility just as Ryder was. But hadn't he always wished he and his sister had come first in his father's life?

He turned onto his back and stared up at the ceiling, unsettled.

"Waah!"

He sat up, surprised to hear Ryder crying as though he knew his father had turned away.

"I'm here for you, Ryder Dawson. Always. That is a promise."

That whispered declaration didn't stop the crying. In fact, Ryder's cheeks were getting red and he looked spitting mad.

Colt knew enough about the fussing by now to quickly pick up the baby instead of giving him a minute to settle. He turned on the bedside lamp and headed over to the changing table, making quick work of the soggy diaper. Not only did the crying stop, but he made no rookie movies. Feeling quite proud of himself, he still managed to get a foot in the jaw when he went to pick Ryder back up.

"Thanks, bud," he said with a grin. "That felt

good. I love a good kick in the face at three in the morning."

Ryder seemed to like the movement, being picked up, being laid down, a little action of getting his diaper changed and some cornstarch sprinkled, picked up again, but now he was crying once more. "Hmm. Got some gas in that little belly of yours? I'm going to try Ava's trick of the bicycle legs."

He brought Ryder over to the bed and laid him down, pumping his chubby little legs, and the baby did stop crying. He batted his arms and smiled, his eyes getting droopy.

"Hey, I'm getting okay at this," he whispered. "I told you everything was going to be fine, right? I meant it even if I thought it involved my relatives taking better care of you than I could. But I'm getting there, Ryder."

He might not want to think about all Ava had said earlier tonight, but he was fine with remembering how she'd let him handle things last night. Smart woman, smart move. He'd wanted her to rush in and save him, save the day. And she had by closing the door in his face.

He had a lot to learn from Ava Guthrie.

He flashed back to their kiss. Kisses. The feel of her against him, the scent of her hair and skin.

Colt picked up Ryder again and paced the room, rubbing his back, then slid him into the crook of his arm to lull him back to sleep. He walked over to the window, swaying side to side a bit, and could just make out half the giant wreath he'd hung high up on the barn after dinner.

He'd climbed down the ladder and she was waiting with Ryder in her arms, the look on her face at the sight of the wreath worth the hell it had been getting it up there.

He wanted to make her smile. He wanted to give her the Christmas she deserved.

He wanted *her*. And that was another line of thinking he had to quit.

Chapter Ten

The next day, Ava was in the kitchen stirring the pitcher of iced tea she'd made for lunch with Vivi and Maria when she heard a car coming up the drive.

The sound reminded her of the last time she'd heard a vehicle coming, going out to find Colt Dawson behind the wheel of his fancy black SUV. Asking questions. *A* question.

That felt like eons ago. But it had been just days.

She put on her down jacket and headed out to greet them, the alpacas in their pasture looking up at the sound of the doors and inching closer to the gate in case there was a treat coming.

"Of course we have treats for you girls!" Vivi called as she got out of the car, her shoulder-length red hair glowing in the afternoon sunshine. Ava would say she was in her late forties. "You think we'd come to our favorite alpaca ranch without apples and carrots?"

"We've missed you, darling gals," Maria added, waving a baggie of treats. Maria was around sixty with a dark pixie and sparkling dark eyes behind red-frame glasses.

Aw. They were clearly such kind, warm women. Ava instantly felt bad that she hadn't invited them before now.

As they all arrived at the fence, Maria asked, "Okay to give them a little love? Iris always let us spoil these darlings."

Ava smiled. "Of course."

Once the treats were chomped, Vivi and Maria looked around.

"Wow," Vivi said. "The ranch looks so festive. We were oohing and ahhing as we came up the drive."

"The wreath on the barn—so beautiful!" Maria said. "And the garland. With the snow on the ground and the roofs, it's like a Christmas wonderland."

"You've done an amazing job here, Ava," Vivi added. "I can't put my finger on it, but the entire place just looks refreshed."

"I've been working hard," Ava said. "But I admit I'm lucky that I'm bartering with a cowboy. He's done a lot of repair work and got that giant wreath up there," she added, pointing to the barn.

"I tell everyone—what every woman needs is a cowboy," Maria said with a wink.

Ava laughed—though she absolutely agreed—and they headed inside.

Maria put her quiche Lorraine in the oven to heat up and Vivi gave them a peek of the pumpkin pie she'd made and Ava served the iced tea. They sat at the table, Maria's dark eyes going straight to the baby bottles on the counter.

"Okay, call me nosy, but is there a baby here? I can't resist a baby and I have six grandchildren—all under three."

Ava grinned. "The bartering I mentioned? The cowboy is a widowed father. The baby is just four months and precious."

"Oh gosh," Vivi said. "Four months and lost his mama?"

Somehow, when these kind, warm, chatty women were talking about it, she suddenly saw the situation only from Ryder's point of view, and her eyes welled with tears. "We've known each other a long time so we're helping each other out. It is wonderful to have a baby in the house."

Vivi patted her hand.

Maria put her arm around Ava's shoulder and gave a squeeze. "Well, we won't ask the details since there are clearly *details*, but I'm glad you both have help—especially at Christmas."

Vivi nodded. "We love details, but hey, you don't know us yet. In a week, you'll spill it all." She laughed her great throaty laugh. "I'm gonna grab the quiche."

A few minutes later, they were eating, talking, laughing, drinking, and Ava felt as light as alpaca fleece. She wished she'd invited Vivi and Maria before today but she was just darn glad they were here now. She hadn't even realized how starved she was for female company.

Vivi cut into her slice of quiche. "I'm so glad you got in touch, honey. We tried to keep up the knitting circle just Maria and me, but it wasn't the same without Iris."

"And the alpacas as our view," Maria added. "We always sat in the living room by the sliding glass doors so we could look up anytime and see their funny faces."

"So Iris was part of the group and not more like the instructor?" Ava asked.

Vivi took a sip of her iced tea. "Well, she started out as the instructor and for a solid year, I'd say, she was definitely in teacher mode. But by the second year, when Maria and I were intermediate knitters, she began joining in the conversation—

offering advice and her no-nonsense wisdom as we—Vivi and I—talked about every little personal thing going on in our lives. By the third year, I'd say we all became true friends."

Did that mean Iris had opened up to them?

Maria put down her fork. "I really miss her."

"How long was the knitting group going on?" Ava asked, wishing she could have been a part of it.

"Four years?" Maria said, looking at Vivi. "Or was it five?"

"I think five," Vivi said.

"I'm so glad she had you two," Ava said. "I don't get the sense she had many friends. And I guess you know she didn't speak to her family."

Maria nodded. "She mentioned that a couple times, around holidays that first year when we'd ask if she was traveling for Christmas, but she'd always just shake her head and say she was on her own. 'Me and the gals,' she'd say."

On her own.

So unnecessarily! Or maybe not. Ava didn't know why her aunt had chosen to cut herself off. Her mother always said Iris was just a certain kind of person, a loner, who preferred animals to people and that was just the way she was made and that they shouldn't take it personally.

She had so many questions for Vivi and Maria and they were clearly very open and gabby, but she didn't want to put Iris's dear friends, these two women who really seemed to care about her, on the spot or make them uncomfortable. She'd wait a bit and see how the talk unfolded.

"Iris really was one of a kind," Maria said. "I don't think I'd ever met anyone like her. No nonsense but with a fun streak. Though, I'll tell you, took a while for that side of her to come out with us. She was all knit one, purl two for a *long* time."

Vivi smiled. "She really was. But oh, when she finally started feeling more comfortable with us, she gave great advice. If it wasn't for Iris Ludlow, I might be divorced. For a woman who'd never married, she sure knew a lot about marriage."

"Wisdom. Iris had it."

Ava was inhaling all this wonderful information. "I wish I'd been a part of her life. But she didn't want anything to do with her family and I have no idea why. She estranged herself when I was just a kid."

The two women looked at each other.

"She talked about you a couple times over the years," Vivi said. "She said 'I only met that little girl once but I could tell she had spunk.'"

"Spunk?" Ava almost snorted. "I don't think anyone's ever used that word to describe me."

"Are you kidding?" Maria said. "Spunk is inheriting an alpaca ranch and doing a great job when you had no experience with alpacas or ranching. Your aunt was right."

Huh. "I hadn't thought of it that way." She put her fork down and looked from Vivi to Maria. "Thank you so much for all this. It means so much to me."

"I don't know the details of why she distanced herself from her only family," Maria said. "She wouldn't talk about it. She wouldn't talk about herself at all. But just know it had nothing to do with you."

Ava took that in. "I appreciate that. I wish I knew more about her life. I found a photo of her with a young man—in the sweater she was wearing when she was taken into the hospital. The back of the photo said 'Iris and Jack. Hopper's Lake. August.' Did she ever talk about him? Do you know who he was?"

They both shook their heads. "She definitely didn't show us the photo," Vivi said. "And she never mentioned a Jack. In the years we knew her, twice a week every week, she never talked about her love life. Ever. We asked, trust us."

Ava had no doubt about that. If these two hadn't been able to get Iris's story out of her, no one could.

So who was Jack? And what happened between them?

Vivi put down her fork, her expression wistful as if she was remembering something. "She did say one personal thing early on when we'd pester her about her life story. I suppose it was explanation in itself. She said, 'I went through something that changed how I looked at things, changed me, irrevocably.'"

Ava gasped.

"I remember that, too," Maria said. "I'll never forget the way she said *irrevocably*. Something happened and that was that."

"I wonder what," Ava said. "Something to do with Jack?"

"I'm not proud of this," Maria said, "but like I said, I'm nosy. And I cared about Iris very much. So I pulled her aside one day and asked her if she wanted to talk about whatever happened. I said I'd been through some very difficult times and maybe I could help.

"She said, 'Dear Maria, it wasn't any kind of tragedy. Just a run-of-the-mill thing that happens to many. But it changed me. Let's just leave it at that.'"

Ava realized she was staring hard at Maria. "I'm so relieved to hear it wasn't a tragedy. My mind was going in so many sad directions."

"I think she got her heart broken bad," Vivi said. "Happens all the time. And to everyone, no matter who you are."

"Probably," Maria said.

Ava nodded. Just a run-of-the-mill broken heart, as if there was anything ordinary or everyday about a broken heart. Ava knew all about that.

"And Iris also said, a time or two when I'd pester her to join me for Christmas or her birthday, 'I'm fine right here. I've got my ranch and my alpacas and a nice business going. Everything is A-OK.'"

"Well, that makes me feel better," Ava said, cutting a bite of quiche as her appetite came back. "That she was content, if not happy."

"She did seem content," Maria said. "This place was everything to her. Almost like all she needed."

Ava frowned and put down her fork. "I wonder why she turned away from family, though. She had a niece and a great-niece, some cousins."

Maria shrugged. "Some people just turn inward. She definitely isolated herself. But she had her groups—us, acquaintances in town, the feed store, auctions. She belonged to some online alpaca groups. She wasn't a hermit. She just liked to be on her own."

Vivi nodded. "She put on a lot of programs, particularly for children, and earned good money with that. She was a good businesswoman and her devotion to the alpacas really shone through. We didn't know the ranch was suffering financially. Or that she'd put on the Christmas festival to try and save it."

Maria took a sip of her tea. "In the hospital she'd admitted she'd spent her last penny on hay but at least she hadn't had to sell any of her girls and that her great-niece was going to take care of the ranch. She said she knew that in her heart and soul just from that one time she'd met you as a girl."

Ava gasped for the second time. "She said that?"

Maria nodded. "She said she gave the nurse your name and that you lived in a town called Bear Ridge and that the minute you heard she was in the hospital and that it didn't look good, you dropped everything to rush out here to be by her side."

Ava remembered that. She'd been home when her landline had rung, and it rarely rang.

"I only had two days with her," Ava said. "And she'd been so frail and weak that she was barely able to talk. But I'm glad she knew I'd take care of the ranch. She didn't even ask me to, now that I think about it."

Ava froze. She thought about how Colt's father had made him promise to give up his dream for Bertrand's own. But Iris hadn't even asked. She'd just left her the ranch—and the decision, what to do with it—completely up to her.

Oh, Aunt Iris, she thought, tears welling again.

"She knew in her heart, mind and soul that you'd take care of her ranch and her gals. She just knew. And you have."

The tears started coming and Ava swiped at her eyes. Both women leaped up to hug her.

"I'm okay," she said. "I didn't know any of this. Thank you both. You have no idea."

"We'd do anything for you, honey," Maria said. "You're like having our Iris back."

"Does that mean you'll teach me to knit?" Ava asked. "Now that I have help around here for the next couple of weeks, I can take some time to myself. Then I'll be ready to teach a fiber arts knitting workshop come spring."

Both women beamed. "We'll teach you today," Vivi said.

As Ava served the pie and poured coffee, she asked about the Christmas festival and how it had gone. The answer: not well.

"The first year was successful enough, but the ranch was too run-down last Christmas and Iris wasn't well, so she kind of put people off. Just a handful of people showed up. She didn't really do much advertising, though. We offered to help but she kept putting us off with an 'Eh, maybe I won't do it again this year. So much trouble.'"

"We wished we'd known she was ill," Vivi said. "For a long while she'd just say she was under the weather and we didn't realize she was getting sick."

"I'm just so glad you two were there for her," Ava said.

And me, too, she thought, so grateful with what they'd told her about Iris knowing she'd take care of her ranch. Without asking. She'd never known her aunt, but somehow, her aunt had known *her*.

A half hour later, over coffee and pumpkin pie, Ava finally learned to knit. Or was trying to learn, anyway. The wooden needles were clumsy in her hands, and she kept using the tail to knit with and her stitches were uneven. But she was trying. And she liked the yarn—from one of the ranch's alpacas, she wasn't sure which. A beautiful deep green shade that Vivi said had been a top seller in knitting shops across Wyoming.

"You'll get it," Maria assured her, peering at her stitch work.

Vivi nodded. "And then you'll wonder how you ever lived without knitting. Instant Christmas presents, too. Once you're comfortable to start a project, you can make a simple scarf. Easy-peasy."

Ava smiled, trying to pick up the next loop, which had somehow gotten so tight on the needle she was having trouble getting the needle in. At least she knew what she was giving Colt for Christmas. Even if she wouldn't see him wear it after the twenty-fifth.

Something was bothering Ava, Colt was pretty sure. A few hours ago, he'd come in on the tail end of her lunch with Iris's knitting circle and had met Vivi and Maria. He'd been holding Ryder, and they'd made quite a fuss over the baby. Over him, too.

When they'd left, they'd promised to not only

attend the Christmas festival but tell everyone they knew about it. Ava had seemed happy—for the company, especially friends of Iris's—but now she looked a bit down.

He'd knocked on her bedroom door once earlier since she'd been scarce since they'd left, but she said she was just doing some thinking and he let her be. He'd wanted to just go right in and hold her, listen to her, but he got the sense she needed to be alone. Now she was sitting on the living room sofa, her laptop on one side of her and a ball of green yarn on the other, knitting needles in her hands.

"Look," she said, holding out her work. "I've almost got a pot holder. This is made from alpaca fleece. I'm not sure from which of our gals."

"Did Iris use to have a green alpaca?" he asked with a grin. "Kidding."

She offered a little smile. "On my list is to learn the whole process of how alpaca fleece is turned into yarn. For now, I'm determined to get better at this," she added, frowning at her pot holder, which had a little hole toward the center, one end crooked. "Oh—I finished a draft of the flier for the festival. Want to see?"

"Sure do." A cry came from upstairs, and he

barely flinched, let alone moved. He waited a beat, then another. Silence.

"I'm determined to get better at *that*, and looks like I have," he said with a smile. "The old Colt would have beelined up the stairs to check on Ryder." He looked at her, tilting his head. "You okay? You seem down."

"I'm all right. Just a lot on my mind. I learned a lot today—nothing bad, actually. Just…heavy on the heart." She put the needles and square green thing to the side, then put her computer on her lap. "The good news is that the flier makes even me want to attend the festival, so that's got to be a good sign."

"I'm here if you want to talk, Ava. You know that, right?"

She looked at him and nodded. "I know."

He sat beside her. "So let's see the flier."

She opened the document, which was well designed and easy to read. "Once I finished creating the flier, I added this to the bottom," she said, pointing. "*In memory and honor of Iris Ludlow, founder of Prairie Hills Alpaca Ranch.* I think she'd like that."

"I think so, too."

"So folks can come by any time between eight in the morning and three thirty—because it'll get dark by four thirty—and take walking tours of the ranch, meet the alpacas and pet them, learn about alpacas in posted signs like zoos have— Iris actually made those herself—and then they can stop at the crafts tables and make a Christmas ornament using alpaca fleece. Vivi and Maria are going to supervise the craft tables so that I can stay by the alpacas' pasture and give a little talk about them, answer questions, make sure no one's feeding them bubble gum or chocolate."

"Good idea," he said. "Sounds like a really great day."

"And here I list the complimentary refreshments—Christmas cookies, which Vivi and Maria had offered to make tons of—apple cider and eggnog. And everyone can take a photograph with their favorite alpaca since I found Iris's instamatic camera and it still works. All for the price of five bucks per person, children free."

"The event is great. But I don't think you need to charge entry the way your aunt felt she had to. You want people to come to this wonderful community event, and people like *free* especially when they're spending a ton already on Christmas gifts. I've got you covered for the festival and it doesn't even sound like you'll need all that much."

He wouldn't mention that he'd placed some orders for the ranch, too, everything from hay to the pellets that supplemented the alpacas' diet to a local company to come out and redo the back fence line. Some would arrive before Christmas, some after. He figured while he was here, he was here. His money included.

"And come spring," he added, "when you post fliers and ads for the workshops and summer camps, everyone will remember the beautiful alpaca farm where they made ornaments and drank eggnog and touched an alpaca's nose and they'll register in droves."

"Helps having a businessman around," she said with a smile. "You're absolutely right."

He grinned. "I thought I wasn't a CEO here."

"You're definitely not. But all that experience is very useful, so I'll take it." She laughed. I get three Colts in one—the CEO, the cowboy and a true friend. Someone I can really talk to." Her cheeks got a little flushed as if she hadn't meant to say that last part.

"You're giving me a lot more than I'm giving you," he said, looking into her beautiful hazel eyes. "Trust me."

"Like what?" she asked.

"Like my sanity. Like every old dream I had

to be wearing a cowboy hat and working the land. Like the truth. And the opportunity to be a good father. I'm getting all that. In one absolutely lovely person named Ava Guthrie."

"I think we're even," she whispered.

He couldn't take his eyes off her face. She was still looking at him, too.

And before he could even think about what he was doing, stop himself, he was kissing her. She was kissing him.

He felt her hands tugging up his shirt, and off it came, then hers was next. He groaned at the sight of her lacy white bra, her soft skin.

Now her hands were on the snap of his jeans, pulling down the zipper, her soft hand slipping inside.

"Ava," he said on a moan, closing his eyes.

He kissed a line across her neck, down her collarbone, down to the curve of her breasts. She smelled very faintly of flowers. He couldn't get enough of her, get close enough to her.

He took off her bra, his hands exploring, his mouth following. As she trailed her lips on his neck, in his ear, he got out of his jeans, his boxer briefs flung on the floor.

He looked into her eyes and gently tugged each side of her leggings, needing them off now, needing access. She looked right back at him and slid them down her creamy legs.

Now all she had on was little white cotton underwear with tiny blue flowers and he could barely take it. He kissed her deeply, then moved his mouth straight down to her breasts, down to her stomach until he inched off all that was keeping him from her.

He felt her hand reach around his erection and he almost lost it but closed his eyes for control.

"You are so beautiful," he whispered.

"You, too," she whispered back before claiming his mouth with her own.

He couldn't wait any longer. He kept his eyes on her lovely face as he hovered over her. "Complicated," he whispered. "Are you sure?"

"Very," she whispered back.

And then he made love to Ava Guthrie, forgetting what made this complicated, forgetting everything but how good she felt, how in sync they were, how he never wanted this to end.

Chapter Eleven

Colt woke up in the dark, the silence ensuring that it wasn't a cry from Ryder that jolted him from a deep sleep. No, it was the woman lying close beside him on the couch, her head on his chest.

Ava.

He reached for the big throw across the top of the sofa and covered them. Half of him wanted to stay where he was, just like this, forever. The other half wanted to bolt. Since he couldn't even sit up without waking her, he would stay put.

Tough job, he thought, shaking his head at himself.

Everything about sex with Ava was incredible. He'd expected it to be need-based and almost kind of solemn but it wasn't like that at all. It had been explosive and *fun*. She'd gotten on top. She'd nibbled his ear and whispered things into his ear. They'd been lying down, they'd sat up.

They'd made love *twice*.

Oh, how I needed this, she'd said at least three times. Him, too.

He closed his eyes on a deep, satisfied sigh.

The big art deco clock on the wall said it was just past five in the morning. The sky was dark. Not a peep from upstairs.

"So this wasn't a dream," a sleepy voice said.

He wrapped his arms around her. "Oh, it was."

She grinned. "I wasn't expecting that. I don't know what I was expecting, but not what actually went *on* on this old sofa."

He laughed. "I know what you mean. Guess we're just full of surprises."

Her whole face was lit up—happy, satisfied. But when she laid her head back on his chest, her hand reaching up to his shoulders, he got that feeling again, the one making him want to run.

He'd had no business getting romantically involved with Ava. For so many reasons.

He thought what was between them was complicated *before*?

"I'll go make coffee," he said, his voice sounding more strained than he was going for. Which had been natural. Casual.

She lifted her head and looked at him, her hazel eyes searching. "Okay," she said.

But he'd seen in her eyes what she'd wanted to say. *You regret this, don't you?*

Regret wasn't the right word. He just wasn't sure what was.

He reached for his jeans and got them on, then his shirt, and stood up, Ava pulling the throw more tightly around herself.

"I'll go make that coffee," he said.

She bit her lip.

He went into the kitchen, mentally punching himself in the stomach. *Don't make her feel like this was a mistake. That you do regret it. That it was wrong.*

But wasn't it a mistake? Was it?

He filled up the carafe, not sure how the hell he felt. He just knew he needed some air, some space, that his collarless shirt felt like it was squeezing his neck.

He set the coffee to brew, then called out, "I'll go check on Ryder," and practically ran up the stairs.

He stopped halfway down the pink hallway. Then turned around and went back downstairs. Ava had gotten dressed and was standing in front of the window beside the tree, looking out, her face strained.

And he'd put that strain there. She deserved better than that.

He walked up behind her and wrapped his arms around her. "I'm sorry," he said.

She put her hand on his arm and leaned against him. "It's okay. I'm freaked out, too. Just trying not to show it. Better to be honest about it." She turned around and put both hands on his face. "We're both dealing with a lot. Last night happened. And yes, *we* would be very complicated. Not to mention the fact that you're leaving on Christmas Day, Colt. So that takes care of that anyway."

He nodded because he wanted to acknowledge that it did; his end date made having to even think of them as having a future out of the realm of possibilities. He was leaving. Going back to work. Back to his life, two hours away.

But the thought of leaving, of walking out that door with his and Ryder's bags, felt as strange as staying did.

The coffee maker dinged, and they headed into the kitchen.

"Ryder's still sleeping?" she asked, getting out two mugs.

"I didn't get to the nursery. I just turned back around to talk to you."

She put the mugs down and came over and wrapped her arms around him. "You're a good man, Colt Dawson. Whatever happens here, just know you're a good man."

He wasn't sure about that. Or anything.

She went back to the counter and poured the coffee, then brought it over to the table. "I never got the chance to tell you about my conversation with Vivi and Maria about Iris."

"I was wondering if that was why you seemed a bit down after they left."

"What they told me actually made me feel better," she said, adding cream to her mug. "I guess I was just taking it all in. Even though I didn't learn all that much about Iris, I feel like I understand her better. But after meeting twice a week for five years, she told them very little about herself."

"Really?" he asked. "In five years?" He took a sip of the strong, hot coffee, desperately needing it. "Now that I think about it, I had an uncle like that. He was married but his wife was similar though not to the same degree. Very private, never shared a personal story, never asked questions. That's just the way some people are, I guess."

"They said it took her two years just to even respond to anything personal they said. But she did offer up a few things. She said she'd only met me once, when I was a little kid, but she knew I had spunk—isn't that funny?"

"Funny? You do have spunk. I'm not surprised that your aunt saw that in you as a kid."

Her whole face brightened. "I've never thought of myself that way. But I suppose turning around a failing alpaca ranch is a little spunky." She laughed. "Huh."

"A lot spunky," he said. She definitely didn't give herself enough credit.

"She also said that she went through something that changed her irrevocably. She wouldn't say what, just that it wasn't tragic."

"That's a relief to know," he said, sure that if it had been Ava might be haunted by it.

"But it had to be a big deal. Something that cut her to her core. I think it had to do with a man. Something happened with the two of them that caused her to put walls up around her."

I know how that is, he thought, taking a long sip of coffee. He glanced out the window at the gray-and-purple sky, dawn just starting to break over the mountains. Something happened and now part of him felt numb and part of him felt made of brick.

"I think Iris got her heart broken." She explained about the photograph she'd found in Iris's sweater. "What's so perplexing is that those last weeks she must have known she was very sick. She likely looked for that photo and put it in the pocket of her favorite everyday cardigan and it gave her strength or comfort to know it was there. If he broke her heart to the point that she cut herself off from everything to live out here, why would she keep it close like that?"

"Good question," he said. "Iris was a mystery."

She nodded. "Definitely. I just wish I could unravel it."

"Well, she's in every nook and cranny of this place. So you've got her all around you. Her story may take time to come out, but I'll bet it will."

Her pretty face brightened "How do you always know what to say to make me feel better about everything?"

"Me? I don't think anyone's ever said *that* to me in my life."

"Well you just made me feel tons better. And you made me feel better before when you came back down and hugged me."

He reached across the table and squeezed her hand.

"Vivi and Maria made me realize she was out here living life her way, on her terms. For whatever reason, she was done with people and cut herself off from everyone but she was just fine on her own with her dear alpacas and her own company."

Like I'll be. Exchanging the alpacas and his own company for his son, of course. After the bombshell dropped on his head the other day, he could see why someone would swear off relationships and move to the middle of nowhere.

What his late wife had done made him never want to bring anyone new into his life again. He knew he could trust his family. And Ava *seemed* trustworthy. But he never would have expected subterfuge of the level Jocelyn had gone to.

He'd stay on his own.

Another reason not to give in to his attraction, these feelings for Ava, his inability to resist her. He was done with all that. Love, marriage. Ryder would grow up with all his aunt and uncles, lots of cousins his age.

But Colt was done.

Ava took one of her pushpins out of the little tin box and secured the festival flier to the bulletin of the Prairie Hills town hall. She and Colt—with Ryder surveying the world from the carrier on his daddy's chest—had come into town this morning with a stack of them and they'd hit around ten bulletin boards so far. From the library to the grocery store to the feed store to the dog run in the park.

Had either of them brought up last night? Nope. Not one word. She had the sense that Colt neither regretted it nor thought it had been a good idea. Ava was more in the *I'm glad we did it but now I can't stop thinking about him* camp. Remembering. Maybe now that they had slept together, that constant awareness and tension would dissipate and they could get on with the next two weeks, make good on their deal, plan the festival.

Had that ever worked in the history of time? She wasn't sure how Colt was being affected, but she had never been so aware of him.

"That makes ten fliers posted," he said. He then launched into a rundown to Ryder of everywhere they'd been so far. This was a man focused on the task—not the woman beside him. As linked as the two were, his mind was not on last night.

So get yours back in the game, she ordered herself. *Festival. Save the ranch. Alpacas. Great-Aunt Iris.*

"That's right, Ryder!" she said too cheerily

to the baby. "And next we'll hit the coffee shop. Their bulletin board is the size of a bathtub."

They were both overdoing the "ignore last night" tactic, but they did have a job to do, so Ava figured it was best to go with it. There would come a time when they *couldn't* act like last night had never happened. And then they'd talk about it.

All that a bit more settled in her heart, she straightened the stack of fliers she held, ready to move on, literally and figuratively. Before they'd left the house, Ava had posted on social media with links to the ranch website where the flier was front and center below the photo of the alpacas. She'd hash-tagged the heck out of it and when she'd returned to the house from her morning chores and getting the alpacas into the pasture, her posts had been liked and shared and retweeted—including by two radio stations and three TV stations—so many times.

Yes! she'd thought. *This is what I should be focusing on. Not how up in the air I feel about Colt and where we stand.*

Which was absolutely nowhere. There wasn't even a word to describe their relationship to each other or how they'd come together.

"Onto the bathtub-sized bulletin board," he

said. "And then we can go up that side of the street and see what we may have missed down any side streets."

Prairie Hills might be a small town but it was the county seat, so the downtown was more bustling than she'd expected when she'd arrived. There was a diner, at least six restaurants, including two on the fancy side, a big grocery store and the usual array of businesses. Plus there was a town square with its own community bulletin board—their first stop on the flier tour. The town was a lot like Bear Ridge and probably why she'd felt comfortable here from the get-go.

She didn't get into town often, just to do a big grocery shopping once a month and to look through the feed store for what the alpacas might need, so she'd missed the town being decorated for Christmas. It was so picture-postcard. All the shops were sparkling with lights, the light posts wrapped in red and green garland, and the tree at the town square festooned with white lights that would turn on at dusk. Downtown looked magical, and it gave Ava an extra boost about the festival attracting residents. The sidewalks were busy with people, a few wearing Santa hats, holding many bags and wrapped packages. She hoped all

these people—and their friends and families—
would come to the festival in two weeks.

Inside the coffee shop, Ava posted her flier on
the huge bulletin board near the door, then she
and Colt sat down with their coffees and treat,
Ryder transferred to Colt's lap. Even though it
was cold out, they'd both been in the mood for
iced lattes and were splitting a blondie.

"Aw, what a cutie!" a middle-aged woman said,
her gaze on Ryder, as she was passing their table.
"Wow, he looks just like Daddy."

Ava could see Colt freeze. Luckily the woman
kept walking and didn't just stand there to make
chitchat. Uncomfortable chitchat.

Colt glanced down at the baby on his lap. "He
doesn't look like me at all. And we know why that
is," he added, bitterness creeping into his voice.

"Coloring goes a long way into fooling the
eye," she said. "Particularly with young babies."

He was quiet for a moment, then said, "When
I'd come home from work, sometimes very late,
and Ryder would be awake because of his baby
hours, I would just stare at his face, thinking he
was my mirror image."

Ava sipped her coffee. "I thought so, too, the
day he was born and I got to hold him in the hospital. I even said so to Jocelyn."

"The deception," he said on a harsh whisper. "I don't know that I'll ever get over that."

Ava swallowed. She understood. But bitter for life over something he couldn't change would only hurt him—and possibly Ryder. That was another thing she'd have to work on with him during the short time they had left. He couldn't let it destroy his trust in people. Or love.

And right now, it was doing just that.

Colt ran a gentle hand over Ryder's wispy hair. "He doesn't look all that much like Jocelyn, but again, it's hard to tell because she had brown hair and green eyes. I guess we'll see how his features change with the months."

Months. Months from now, Ava would be standing in the barn, waiting for spring, missing Colt and Ryder.

Ava split their blondie in half, not really tempted by it anymore.

"I wonder about the donor," he said. "The info Jocelyn got on him from the sperm bank or fertility clinic must be somewhere in the house in Bear Ridge. Though I'm surprised I didn't come across it while going through her things."

"What would you want to know?" she asked.

"I have no idea. Maybe I don't want to know anything." He grabbed his latte and took a long sip. "I really *don't* want to know anything but at the same time…" He dropped his head forward.

She reached a hand out to touch his. "I can understand that."

"I can't imagine where she would have kept it—" He froze again. "The safe-deposit box. A couple of weeks ago, I got a call from our bank that she had a box there. The woman said it had been prepaid for five years but if I didn't want to keep the box myself she would refund me. I didn't even connect it until now. Maybe it's where she stashed the paperwork from the fertility clinic."

"She never mentioned that, so I don't know. But it's likely. I don't think she would have dared kept anything to do with all that in the house."

"I guess I'll clear out the box when I get back to Bear Ridge. I'm in no rush to see the paperwork. Or more about the donor. *If* there's more. If there's a photo, I don't want to see it." He leaned his head back. "I'll bring Haley with me to look through it all first."

"Good idea." He wouldn't be able to unsee a photo and she had no doubt he'd be bothered by it. But she definitely didn't remember Jocelyn ever saying *she'd* seen a photo. She had a description of the coloring only because of checked boxes and a written description in the donor's own words.

He changed the subject to the festival, to the crafts tables and what Ava would need for that. If she made a list, he said, she could hang out here with Ryder and he could go pick everything up.

He needed some space, she realized. Some time with his own thoughts, even if he was trying not to think about the truth behind Ryder's paternity. He needed air and to pace.

She'd gone through Iris's office looking for supplies from last year and there were a ton of leftover little wooden cutouts in the shape of alpacas with prepunched holes at the top that kids could color on and attach the alpaca fleece to. Most of the washable markers were dried out and many colors were missing. Iris had a big box full of twisty ties to serve as hangers and different-color fleece that had sticky tabs so no glue required.

She pulled out her phone and texted Colt a brief list of the art supplies. Closer to the date of the festival, they could come back to buy the cider and eggnog. She'd also like to buy the ingredients for Vivi and Maria to make the Christmas cookies so the cost wouldn't fall on them.

He scanned the text he'd just received from her. "Got it. You're okay here for a bit?" he asked, standing up.

"Absolutely," she said.

He was gone in a flash. Oh yeah, the man had definitely needed air.

"Aw, your baby is so adorbs!" a woman passing by holding two coffee cups said. "I'm pregnant," she added, her face beaming. "Our little one is coming this summer. Don't worry—this one is decaf," she added, holding up one of the coffees. She kneeled down a bit to see Ryder. "You are too sweet. And wow, he looks just like you—shape of the eyes, around the mouth. And definitely the nose. He must have Daddy's coloring." With that rush of words and comments, she was on her way to her own table.

Ava mentally shook her head. "Ryder, honey," she said to the baby, "you definitely don't have my eyes, mouth or my nose," she whispered. She'd have to tell Colt about that one, and he'd see how meaningless and throwaway a comment it was. People just made nice—or rude—small talk, no idea that they could be throwing a grenade into someone's latte and blondie.

She watched the woman sit down across from a man, their wedding rings shining, and Ava felt that pang start in her chest. Once upon a time, she just assumed she'd have a husband and a baby, two or three babies, actually. She'd thought she'd found the husband, a good guy who knew she couldn't have children, and she'd never really know if he'd been using that as an excuse not to marry her at the last minute or what. They hadn't been a perfect match, but every time she tried to address their issues, big and small, he didn't like to talk about subjects he found dull or uncomfortable, like her feelings on certain matters.

They hadn't been right for each other, but Jocelyn had always told her there was no such thing as a perfect match. Her fiancé was handsome, successful, a nice person, and someone to grow old with. That was all Ava had needed to know, her best friend had insisted. There's no fairy tale. You get some parts, but not the whole thing.

Ava had never really bought any of that. She'd always known that life wasn't a fairy tale. But the right person for you? The wrong person? You knew that, too. You overlooked, you rationalized, but you knew. Her fiancé *had* done her a favor by leaving her, heartbreaking as it had been at the time.

"Oh, what a cutie pie," another woman said as she wheeled a stroller with her own baby inside. He looked to be a little older than Ryder. "Six months. How about yours?"

Not mine, Ava thought. And exiting my life very soon.

"He's four months," she said.

The woman launched into a rundown of her son's milestones, from his first tooth to just starting on solid foods. "The time goes as fast as everyone says. I feel like he was just born! Same for you?"

"Oh gosh, look at the time," Ava said. "We'd better get going. Nice talking to you," she added, standing up. Ava really did like chatting with people, always had, but sometimes the most "pleasant" small talk for some people made for painful jabs to the heart for others.

The woman thankfully moved on.

With Ryder strapped into the chest carrier, Ava stuffed the bag with the blondie in her coat pocket and was contemplating how to carry an iced latte in each hand and still have a hand free for Ryder, just as a precaution, when Colt came back.

"I hit up the drugstore, grocery store and the gift shop, but they didn't have everything on your list," he said. "We'll just order the rest online."

"Oh my gosh," the woman with the baby stroller said, coming back over, her gaze going from Colt to Ryder. "Your baby looks just like you!"

Colt looked at Ava and gave her a conspiratorial smile. "He's my mini-me."

"He sure is!" the woman said and went back to her table.

Colt rolled his eyes. "The air and errands did me good. There's something kind of absurd about people saying he looks like me when he's not mine. A stab to the heart and gut because of why he actually doesn't, but still just absurd. So I'm just going to let it go."

"While you were gone, one woman told me she thought Ryder looked like *me*—around the mouth, the shape of the eyes." She shook her head.

"That actually makes me feel better." With three bags from the shops on one wrist, he took their coffees and led the way out. "Let's go post the rest of the fliers. You, me and mini-me."

Ava smiled. Maybe the small talkers were actually helping.

They didn't get two steps out the door before another person commented on how cute Ryder was with his fleece bear ears.

"He looks just like Daddy!" an older woman said, opening and shutting her hands in front of her face to play a quick peekaboo.

"Well, he *is* my son," Colt whispered to Ava.

"He sure is," Ava whispered back, and right

there, in the middle of a busy sidewalk full of holiday shoppers, she fell in love.

And just like her aunt Iris, she knew it was irrevocable.

Ava realized she wasn't breathing, her hand over her mouth, and she sucked in a breath. Was this a Christmas miracle? Was she finally going to get answers about what happened between Iris and Jack? She grabbed her phone and texted Colt.

I know you're just like ten feet away but I can't move. I'm in happy shock. Come see.

He was in her bedroom in two seconds, quizzical look on his handsome face. She handed him the laptop with the email open.

"Whoa," he said, sitting on the edge of her bed and reading it. "Wow."

"I know! I can't believe it."

He set the laptop back on her bed desk. "Married four times. Seven kids? Interesting."

"But Iris was the love of his life! The one who got away. There is a story here, Colt. And I'm finally going to know!"

"I'm not clear on why he'd want to get married at the ranch, though," Colt said. "A tribute to what, exactly?"

"I guess Dylan liked his great-uncle's romantic stories over the years of his true love who wouldn't marry him. Maybe he associates the ranch, Iris, with that romance, with true love. I think it's sweet."

"He married four times after," Colt pointed out. "I don't know."

"Maybe because he believed in marriage. Or romance. Or that it would work *this* time. I don't know. Maybe he always hoped he'd find what he had with Iris with someone else but just never did."

"Maybe," he conceded.

She tilted her head. "I just realized something. It was clearly Iris who broke *Jack's* heart. Not the other way around like I was thinking."

He nodded. "There's a lot packed into that email, Ava. A lot."

There was. Ava scanned the email again. She leaned her head against the pillows. "Sounds like Jack had a close relationship with his great-nephew since he could only confide in Dylan about the one who got away. I'm gonna email him back and invite him and his fiancée over."

"I'll leave you to it, then. I'll get back to the Wilkins Electronics acquisition."

Ava frowned and stared up at him. "I didn't know you were working while you were here."

"Well, hardly working. My VP on the deal asked me to look over his final report, so I'm just giving him some notes."

Why was this such a surprise? She should have figured he was keeping up with the office, even all the way out here on a ranch. Still, her heart felt raw. Because it meant he wasn't fully in on being a cowboy again, being a full-time father. "I thought you were taking a real break. Just focusing on Ryder and yourself."

"Easier said than done, Ava. But I can assure you that since I've been here, I've spent about two hours tops on Godfrey and Dawson."

She bit her lip. She supposed two hours in a few days was barely a blip to a workaholic CEO. Some little piece of her hoped the reintroduction to his old dream would stir something in him so deep down that he'd realize what he'd given up and at what cost. But if Colt didn't want to be looking at a report on that acquisition, he wouldn't be, and she had to remember that. He *wanted* to. And he'd be leaving and going back on Christmas day. She knew this. So why was she holding out the slightest bit of hope that he'd give himself his dream for Christmas?

And stay. Right here.

Now she was going way too far. Letting her own old dreams take her places she'd never be able to go.

Write Jack's great-nephew back and let Colt Dawson go. Literally and figuratively.

"Come tell me when he writes back," he said. "All this is much more interesting than the electronics acquisition."

Anything is, she wanted to yell after him. But what she did know about his company and what CEOs found fascinating?

She closed her eyes for a moment, willing herself to put Colt Dawson out of her mind. For the next five minutes, anyway.

She hit Reply.

Dear Dylan,
You're not going to believe this, but I very recently found a photograph of my great-aunt Iris with a young man at a lake, both smiling, arms around each other. The back said: Iris and Jack. Hopper's Lake. August. My aunt died four months ago, and she had that photograph in the pocket of her favorite cardigan that she was wearing when she was rushed to the hospital. Obviously, Jack was very special to her, but I don't know the story of what happened—or why she rejected his marriage proposal. I'm hoping you can fill me in! I'd love to talk about having your wedding here at the ranch. Why don't you

and your fiancée come on out, and I'll show you around and we can have lunch or dinner? Regards, Ava Guthrie

She hit Send, her heart pounding in her chest. She took the photo of Iris and Jack out of her bedside table drawer and stared at it. *Jack Howard. Why wouldn't Iris marry you? I thought you broke her heart but it was definitely the other way around.*

She hoped Dylan would write back today. Between waiting and the complicated man down the hall, Ava wouldn't have a moment's peace.

Though it was barely four o'clock in the afternoon, Colt lay on his bed, Ryder in the bassinet beside him, peacefully napping after all that earlier fussing and carrying on. Ava had helped out, and once he was on his own with Ryder, he'd used her tips and tricks, some working, some not.

My goodness. Colt had been tested—could he handle this, could he get through the problem that had no solution, and he had. Ryder had tired himself out and finally fallen asleep. Colt just had to wait it out, use the tried-and-true and add some new ones, which he had. Turned out that Ryder seemed to like being held with his head on Colt's left arm instead of his right. No idea why. But he'd calmed after that. And once Colt had started singing "Silent Night," the little eyes finally closed.

He'd been scared spitless to transfer Ryder, sure he'd start bawling. But this time, the baby hadn't. He'd gone right in, his arm curling up beside his head. The chest rising and falling, rising and falling.

Colt had almost passed out with relief.

He moved onto his back, staring out the window, the trees, the mountain range. He was thinking about the email. About Jack Howard.

Four marriages. Seven kids. But it all would have worked out with Iris, the one who got away? Not hardly, as his sister liked to say.

Was he being cynical and bitter? Maybe. But c'mon.

He glanced at his own laptop, which he truly hadn't used much since he'd arrived here. The sight of it actually twisted his stomach. He hadn't wanted to read his VP's report, didn't have the head for it right now and wouldn't tomorrow or the next day, but he'd forced himself. The details bored him, as they always had. The deal was the same as every deal, give or take. How his father had found this all so consuming was beyond Colt.

Sometimes he did fantasize about leaving. Walking way. Telling Brandon Godfrey Jr., whom he liked very much, that the company was his, that the Dawson part was ending from here on in.

But what if Ryder's dream *was* to be CEO of his family corporation, started fifty years ago—seventy-five years when Ryder would come of age to work in the executive office? For a man who'd only wanted to make his living riding a horse across a ranch, it was hard to imagine the corporate life being anyone's dream. He thought about Brandon, his co-CEO, who lived and breathed the company just like their fathers had. The guy could talk shop anytime, anyplace—parties, weddings—his eyes lighting up as he discussed the company, its history, the deals, the issues and fires.

So maybe Ryder would be like that. A born CEO like Brandon Godfrey. If that was his son's dream, he'd support and encourage him every step of the way. If Ryder wanted to be a bronc rider or write Western novels? Same thing.

Maybe like the house, Colt should keep the door open for him. Hang on to the Dawson part of Godfrey and Dawson.

So he was going to toil away at Godfrey and Dawson till he dropped dead just in case?

He closed his eyes, not wanting to think about any of this.

What he needed to do was physical work. He had a short list of repairs left to be done and could tackle one of those.

He shoved his laptop under his pillow and headed out with the baby monitor, wishing Ava had a horse at the ranch. What he would give for a ride across the land. He'd thought about buying a horse and keeping it at a good stable, but every time he started looking into it, he'd see a ranch of his own, a stable of his own, horses of his own, cattle and sheep, and three great dogs. And the idea of being a part-time horseman, like a part-time father, left him cold.

Unsettled, he got his tool belt from the shed outside. He needed to strengthen one of the posts of the fence close to the barn. Monitor in his coat pocket, he got to work, the cold snap of air, the pull on his muscles, the scent of snow and trees and alpacas already working their special magic. His head was clearing.

But then Ava came out in her blue down jacket and pink wool hat, headed toward the barn, and all he could think about was her. Their night on the couch. Their trip into town. Their talks. All he was learning from her. The kisses he always wanted.

She turned and saw him and waved and he waved back, and it took everything in him to stay where he was and not run up to her and just wrap his arms around her, seeking…something he couldn't quite name.

Ava was a little too obsessed with her phone and constantly checking her email to see if Jack's great-nephew had responded. So far, almost an hour later, he hadn't. She was in the barn, spreading out fresh straw for the alpacas, and she almost walked right into the wall because her eyes were on the phone in her hands.

Colt had texted her a few minutes ago that he was going back into town—with Ryder—and would return with a surprise, and now she had two things driving her crazy with anticipation.

Close to an hour later—still no email—she heard the car returning and saw through the window that he had Ryder's baby seat in one hand and a pizza box balanced against his side with the other. She hurried out to take the pizza or the baby, and he handed over the pizza—like a very good daddy.

Yum, the smell! She hadn't had pizza since

she'd been at the ranch. She was a budget grocery shopper and couldn't spend money on takeout. So this was a very worthy surprise. Even the alpacas in the pasture knew something good was in the air; she could see them sniffing. She'd hide some treats in their straw so they wouldn't feel left out.

They went into the house, and with Ryder happy in his swing, dug into the pizza, which was so good she almost fell off her chair. Colt had gotten half plain, half pepperoni, and they both had one of each. As they ate, Colt told her he'd arranged for four long tables and forty folding chairs to be delivered a few days before the festival; the party rental company had holiday tablecloths, so he'd brightly chosen red ones with tiny candy canes. He'd mentioned that when he'd gotten up to get a bottle of wine that Vivi had brought on one of her brief visits soon after Iris's funeral.

Between the anticipation of hearing from Jack's great-nephew and the sweet detail of the tablecloths, let alone the tables and chairs themselves, she got up and practically flung herself at him, wrapping her arms around his strong back.

"Whoa, what's this for?" he asked, setting the bottle on the counter and hugging her back. "It's just pizza."

She laughed. "For *everything*, Colt Dawson. For being you. And yes, for the pizza, which I haven't had in four months. Maybe five. For the craft tables and the candy-cane-dotted festive tablecloths. For the tree. For all the work you've done here. For *being* here."

"I thought I told you that you give me much more," he said. "And more than you know."

She leaned her head against his chest. "Thank you, Colt. Just thank you."

"So let's toast each other our mutual thanks," he said, grabbing the bottle he'd put on the counter.

She grinned and took two wineglasses from the cabinet. He uncorked and poured and they toasted. They finished off one more slice each, which was Ava's record. Her phone was pinging away, which she'd gotten used to—she always had several emails a day in response to her fliers and social media, so at this point she was conditioned not to expect any of the pings to be Dylan Howard. It had been almost two hours without a response and he'd probably get back to her tomorrow.

She grabbed her phone to check, of course, hoping like crazy.

"He emailed back!" she practically screamed.

She shot up out of her chair and paced the kitchen, then opened the email and read it.

Hi Ava,

I'm so glad you wrote back. I wasn't entirely sure if I had the right person or place. I talked to my fiancée—her name's Lindy, by the way—and she's so excited about the idea of getting married at the ranch. She totally gets it, you know? I don't think anyone else would, which is just one of the reasons why I love her.

"Oh my God," she said, looking at Ryder. "I adore him already."

She kept reading.

Our moms and Lindy's three aunts are driving us INSANE about the wedding. We're both twenty-three and really wanted to elope to Vegas to some fun, campy Elvis chapel, but our families would go nuts if they didn't attend a big family wedding, so we thought: what if we secretly "eloped" to the ranch where Great-Uncle Jack's long-lost true love lived. Something about it just feels right to me. Like, if only he could have convinced his Iris to marry him, his whole life would have turned out differently. I don't know. I just know we feel like the getting married at the ranch would feel like a tribute to my great-uncle and to true love. Then we'll get married again at the

big family shindig. If I sound nuts, just ignore, but please don't. Is Friday too soon? Lindy and I are both vet techs in town and get off work at 5:00. Would 7 work?
Cheers, Dylan

Ava dropped down on the chair and read the whole thing to Colt.

"He sounds young," Colt said.

"He sounds *romantic*."

Colt raised an eyebrow. "He didn't say anything about why Iris didn't say yes to his marriage proposal. Maybe Jack was irresponsible or a play-the-field type. Four wives?"

"Uh, a little judgmental. We don't know anything."

"I just don't want you to get your hopes up about some romantic parting, Ava. I don't want you to be disappointed."

She shot him a mock scowl. "I hear you. But I just have a good feeling about this. And I like Dylan. He and his fiancée are vet techs. That means they're animal people. Which means they're *good* people."

He smiled. "I suppose so."

But Ava found herself scanning the email, looking for clues that weren't there about why

Iris didn't accept Jack's marriage proposal. Dylan had to know and he didn't say a peep about it in the email. She emailed back that Friday and 7:00 p.m. was great and see you then, and he immediately responded: Can I bring anything? How about a French baguette from the bakery in town? They're so good, right?

She emailed back that she'd love the French bread.

Friday night could not come soon enough.

Chapter Thirteen

For the next couple of days, Ava noticed that Colt was…distant. He wasn't asking for as much help with Ryder, which was great, but she wasn't sure if that was because he finally knew he could do this on his own or because he was avoiding her. He was always up early and off doing whatever he determined needing doing. A fence repair company had come out, which he'd told her was an absolute necessity and that it was on him. She'd added it to the list of what she owed him. Their barter arrangement covered the festival and basic repairs and cowboy work, but he'd told her the porch steps would require experts, same as the rear line of fence.

Not so bad. Come spring, when her workshops and classes were full, she'd be able to pay him back. And then in the summer, at shearing time, she'd start fresh on Iris's special fiber arts label and have yarns and bedding to offer on the website and to hotels. And if she just broke even, well, that would be fine, too. As long as she didn't get in the red. Where she was right now.

But it was hard to be worried about the future when she was so excited about the present. Tonight. Dylan Howard and his fiancée were due over at seven for dinner. Hopefully Ava would finally learn Iris's story.

Ava was making a pasta dish from a handwritten recipe she'd found in Iris's metal box of recipes that sat on the kitchen counter. Just in case Dylan or Lindy were vegetarian, she was going for a pesto sauce and would serve a tossed salad. And there would be the French baguette. Ava had a few more bottles of wine, so she'd offer one with dinner. They could all toast to the bride-and-groom-to-be. And the couple that never got the chance to be.

Colt helped with dinner, getting out the pots and pans and colanders she'd asked for. He wasn't much of a vegetable chopper or slicer, so she'd taken over that and put him on setting-the-table and arranging-the-candlesticks duty. Ryder seemed to enjoy watching them move around the kitchen, the delicious scents making them all hungry.

As she used a long wooden spoon to stir the fragrant green sauce and taste-test the pasta in the big pot at the back of the stove, Colt sat down at the table to feed Ryder.

And there it was again. The fantasy. Her husband feeding the baby. Wife Ava making a special dinner. Their guests bringing a French baguette from the great bakery in town. A good bottle of wine.

She lost herself in that until the timer dinged on the pasta and she came hurtling back to earth. To reality. That Colt wasn't hers. That Ryder wasn't hers. That they were both leaving in a little over a week.

And that their guests tonight might have information that would disappoint Ava.

Ever the optimist, she lowered the flame on the sauce, decided the pasta could use two more minutes and then dressed the salad. Her timing was pretty good tonight. Probably because she didn't have to worry about setting the dining room table or putting out the candles.

A loud burp came from the table, and Ava laughed. "I'll never get over that tiny body making that huge sound."

Colt smiled. "Same here." He held Ryder against his chest, giving his back a gentle rub, his soft little cheek a kiss.

I am melting in a puddle of goo, she thought so wistfully that she almost sighed aloud.

The sound of a vehicle coming up the drive had her head back on straight. It was just before seven. She glanced out the window to see a small silver car pulling up.

Colt stood, holding Ryder, and when boots could be heard on the porch, they headed to the door, Ava opening it to see a young couple.

"Aw," the pretty young redhead said, her eyes on the baby. "He's so beautiful."

Colt smiled. "His name's Ryder. I'm Colt Dawson."

"And I'm Ava Guthrie."

"Dylan Howard," the tall young man with sandy-brown hair said, pointing at himself with a smile. "And this is my fiancée, Lindy."

Lindy smiled. She had the baguette in one hand and a box with a red ribbon in the other. "We brought bread and the most delicious-looking cake. It's chocolate layer."

"That bakery is amazing," Ava said. "Thanks so much." She'd stopped in to see what they had when she'd first come to town, and she'd treated herself to a cranberry orange muffin that almost melted in her mouth, but finances had meant baking her own breads and treats. "Dinner is ready, so Colt, why don't you show Dylan and Lindy the way to the dining room, and I'll be in in a sec."

As Colt headed toward the dining room with Ryder, Dylan following and chatting about the "beautiful country out here," Lindy whispered to Ava, "I can't wait to be you. Married with a baby in a beautiful ranch house like this."

Ava froze, hopefully not noticeably. "Colt and I aren't married," she said. "The baby is his, actually."

"Oh," Lindy said, her cheeks flushing. "I'm sorry. There I go, making assumptions."

"It was totally natural for you to assume that," she said. "We answered the door together, Colt holding a baby. Of course it seemed like we were a couple who lived here together, so no worries." Hadn't she just been fantasizing about that very scenario moments ago? Husband. Wife. Baby. "Want to grab the salad for me?" she asked to set the young woman at ease.

Lindy smiled with relief and followed Ava into the kitchen. In a minute, they had the platters on the dining room table, and they were all seated, Ryder in his baby swing on the floor in the corner by the window, chewing on his little fabric book.

"I couldn't believe when I saw the flier for the Christmas festival at the coffee shop," Dylan said, forking a bite of salad. "Alpacas always seemed kinda magical to me because of my great-uncle Jack. To know that his true love started an alpaca farm. Does that make any sense?"

"Absolutely," Ava said. "My mother used to collect rocks. Just ordinary rocks she thought were pretty, and any time I'd see a rock, just a plain old rock on the ground, I'd feel it was special. It's the connection when you care about someone."

"Exactly," Dylan said. "And alpacas—I mean, how crazy cute are they?"

"Super cute," Lindy agreed.

"So, Dylan," Ava said. "I'm just going to come right out and ask. Did your great-uncle ever tell you why Iris didn't accept his proposal?"

He put his fork down. "Well, yeah." He glanced around the table kind of uncomfortably. "I mean, it's kind of…personal."

"Ohhh," Ava said, her nerve endings trembling.

Dylan's expression was squeamish. "I just mean, I'm not sure if I should blurt it out over salad and pesto pasta."

Ava liked this young man. He had heart, that was for sure. "Well, maybe we can talk later, you and I. For now, how about you and Lindy tell us what you envision for your wedding. Are you thinking soon? After the new year?"

"We're thinking Christmas Eve," Lindy said, her brown eyes twinkling. "In the morning. It'll be just the two of us, no guests. We have a minister who's agreed to perform the ceremony so we just need permission to hold the wedding here. When we drove up, we immediately both said we'd like to have the ceremony right in front of the alpaca pasture with that cool red barn next to us."

Ava smiled. "You can absolutely have your wedding in that spot. I'll even take pictures, if you like."

Dylan beamed. "Really, so it's a go? Christmas Eve morning?"

"It's a go," Ava said.

The happy couple both leaped up from their seats and wrapped themselves in a hug, both of them actually jumping up and down. *Aw, young love*, Ava mused.

A glance at Colt told her he was charmed by the sweet couple, too. Alpacas? A barn? No guests? Bridezilla, Lindy was not.

"Oops," Lindy said, "we're probably shaking Ryder's baby seat. Sorry."

"He's giggling away," Colt said, "so, I think he liked it."

For a moment, they all watched Ryder laughing, that wonderful big sound coming from the little body, then Dylan and Lindy sat back down.

"So, Dylan, you were close to your great-uncle Jack?" Ava asked, spearing a bite of pasta.

"To be honest, we really weren't all that close. He only had one sibling, a brother, and I'm the only kid, so that's why he spilled his secrets to me when the families would get together for birthdays and holidays. My dad was married to the same woman for like fifty years. Jack had four wives and seven kids, so I guess he felt like I was the only one he could talk to about Iris."

"Did it make you uncomfortable?" Ava asked. "Hearing about them?"

"Nah," Dylan said, twirling a forkful of spaghetti. "He fell crazy in love but she wouldn't marry him. And when he knew no matter what he did she'd never say yes, he moved on. And on. And on."

Ava tried not to smile at his wry humor. "I'm sure he loved his wives, too, though."

"Oh, I think he did in the beginning," Dylan said, "but when your heart belongs to someone else, maybe you can't get past that, you know?"

Ava swallowed. She did know. She was well aware she'd never get past the way she felt about

Colt Dawson. Or Ryder. When they left, they'd take her heart with them.

"It wasn't like your great-uncle just married for the heck of it, though," Lindy said, taking a sip of her wine. "I think he really tried. With every wife. He wanted to find what he felt with Iris. But he just never did."

That was so damned sad. For Jack and for the women he'd married. For his children.

"It's the impression I got every time Dylan would tell me about his uncle's stories," Lindy continued. "I never met Jack, since he passed five years ago, and I've only known Dylan for two years."

"I'll bet you're right," Ava said, glancing at Colt. "That he did try. Hoping to feel that same way."

"What was he like?" Colt asked.

"He was great," Dylan said. "Really nice. Good-natured, funny. Totally devoted to his kids, all bratty seven of them. Six boys and a girl."

Ava smiled. "Wow. That's a lot of boys."

"Oh, trust me," Lindy said, "the girl could kick all their butts."

They all laughed and talked less and ate more, Colt pouring the wine, checking on Ryder, whose eyes were drooping. Lindy talked about her dresses—she had two, of course, one for the secret ranch wedding and one for the big family affair.

"I bought the ranch dress today," Lindy said. "It's tea-length satin and kind of fifties movie star, like Audrey Hepburn. My gown for the family wedding, which will be on Valentine's Day, is all beaded pouf. I love it, too. But I love my secret ranch wedding dress so much."

Ava smiled. When she got engaged, she and Jocelyn had taken road trips to bridal boutiques, Ava trying on so many dresses and never finding The One. She liked many of them, but none of them screamed *say yes to this dress*. Maybe because the guy had been wrong? She'd bought one that was pretty enough, but she never loved it. Not the way a bride is supposed to. The day after her wedding was supposed to happen, Ava carried the long dress bag into her car, threw it in the trunk and planned to dump it in a garbage can and throw dirt on it, but as she'd been about to, she realized she'd feel better knowing it had gone to good use, to a bride who maybe *would* fall in love with it at a bargain price, particularly, and she'd brought it to the local thrift shop, its origins remaining a mystery.

She shook off those memories, focusing on

the conversation. "We'll be your witnesses," Ava said, glancing at Colt.

"That would be great!" Dylan said. "I forgot we need two."

They talked more about the wedding and what they envisioned, a short-and-sweet ceremony, the alpacas right behind them in their pasture, the barn with the big Christmas wreath, true love in the air for thirty years—per Dylan.

Ava smiled to herself. Her aunt likely had carried that love, had in the air all around her, for the past thirty years. If she had that photograph in her pocket, she'd needed it, wanted it, for strength and support, to remember, to say goodbye. She just hoped Iris hadn't been full of regret.

After the pasta, bread and salad were gone, Colt cleared the table and Dylan and Lindy went into the kitchen to get the dessert, Ava keeping an eye on Ryder. After dessert, when Colt took the baby upstairs to get him ready for bed, she'd ask Dylan to tell her what happened between Iris and Jack, why her aunt had turned down his proposal.

And broken both their hearts.

Colt sat in the rocking chair by the window of his room with Ryder nestled in his arms, Ava sitting on his bed, Dylan and Lindy sitting cross-legged on the round rug. Turned out the soon-to-be newlyweds wanted to see the bedtime routine for themselves since they were excited about starting their family. They both wanted two kids and had names picked already: Madeline for a girl and Matthew for a boy.

Colt really wanted to think the couple too young and idealistic and romantic to even exist, but they seemed smart and mature, and were both truly likeable.

"He's a really cute baby," Dylan said, his gaze soft on Ryder. "I can't wait to have kids."

Colt stared at him. "You don't hear that every day from a young guy."

"Right?" Lindy said, taking Dylan's hand and holding it. She gave him a kiss on the cheek. "My Dylan is one of a kind."

Dylan kissed her back. "If I'm half as great to my own kids as *my* dad was—is—to me, they'll be lucky."

"Aw," Ava said, sliding a glance to Colt. "That's so nice."

It was, no doubt about that. A great dad was someone to emulate. Colt had managed to follow in the fatherly footsteps of a workaholic who constantly disappointed his children with his absences.

Dylan seemed lost in thought for a moment. "I believed my great-uncle when he said he didn't care that Iris couldn't have kids—" His eyes widened and he sat very still. "Ugh, I didn't mean to say that. Blurt it out like that. It seemed private. Sorry," he said, looking at Ava.

Colt darted his gaze to Ava, who seemed shell-shocked. He got up with Ryder and sat down next to her on the bed.

She slowly turned to look at him, then at Dylan. "It's okay," she said, and he could tell she was trying to inject a lightness she didn't feel into her voice. "I never got to know my great-aunt. She estranged herself around that time—I was just a little girl. So I'm getting to know her through her friends and now through this great love of hers, your great-uncle. I'm glad you told me."

Colt slid a hand free from around Ryder and took hold of Ava's and she squeezed it back.

Dylan looked relieved. "Jack told me he was a real lughead for telling Iris he wanted a huge family and talking about it so much on their early dates. He was madly in love with her, this fiercely independent woman who worked as a hand on an alpaca farm—they were her favorite animals. He said if he'd known she couldn't have kids, he wouldn't have said anything about children. But it was too late."

"Jack probably thought wanting kids would score him points," Lindy said, her voice wistful. "I mean, it sure did when Dylan told me on our first date that he wanted to have kids young, by the time he was twenty-five."

Colt stared at Dylan, this alien creature of a human. When you had a loving, nurturing dad as a role model, maybe that was what happened: you had kids who wanted to be just like you. And get right to it, too.

"Yup," Dylan said. "But he had no idea. Iris turned down his proposal and said she'd never believe he'd be happy without that big family he always talked about. Jack said he tried to change her mind but she said she was upset enough about her medical condition as it was and to let her go just like she was letting him go."

"Upset," Ava repeated quietly, and he knew Dylan had just unwittingly confirmed something for Ava.

The subject was complex and multilayered and he wished he could talk to Ava about it, hold her, comfort her, but she was focused on Dylan again, intently so.

"He couldn't find her after that," Dylan continued. "She went traveling for a while, but then he heard she'd come back to Prairie Hills and bought a ranch way out in the country and was raising alpacas. He went over to the ranch and got down on one knee right in front of a huge brown alpaca and proposed again. But Iris said no, and he told me he could tell something had changed about her, something in her expression. That she'd never say yes."

The irrevocable change, Colt thought, recalling what Ava told him she'd heard from her knitting group. *She went through something and it changed her irrevocably.*

"I want to cry whenever I hear that part," Lindy said.

Dylan put his arm around her shoulder. "Makes me feel so bad for them. Uncle Jack told me he forced himself to start dating and six months later, he married his first wife."

"Goodness," Ava whispered, her voice so clogged with emotion.

"So that's why we want to get married here," Dylan said. "Right in front of the alpacas. As a tribute to Jack and Iris. If only she'd said yes. If only she'd believed him."

Dammit, even Colt was so moved by the story that his own stone heart felt a pang. Sounded to him like Jack would have given up his long-term wish for a huge family for the woman he loved. Why Iris didn't believe him—if she didn't believe him—was the question.

He glanced at Ava and she looked so sad. He wished he could hold her, even if she wasn't ready to talk about it—and there was a lot to talk about.

"Well, I'd better get this little guy to bed," Colt said, standing. He had a feeling they all could use a little breathing room. The newlyweds-to-be with their own thoughts, clasping their hands in the car, grateful that their own love story wasn't going to be interrupted. Completely halted.

And Ava to let all she'd learned settle inside her. He wanted to be there for her when she wanted to talk about it, speculate, which was really all they could do with the information they had.

"We'd better get going," Lindy said, popping up, as well. "The vet practice we work for opens at seven, so we have to get up early."

Colt was about to say *You don't know early* like a cranky old man, but he kept it to himself. They'd know soon enough. Waking up all night long. Pacing the house with a screamer.

And the ways in which a baby could change you completely, startling you with the depths of your capability to love. But the one thing Colt Dawson knew with absolute certainty in the world? The baby didn't have to be yours biologically to have your heart cracked wide open.

Ava lay in her bed, tossing and turning, fluffing and refluffing her pillow. She turned onto the left side, staring at the photos on her bedside table. The six alpacas in a seashell frame. Her parents and her on the porch of their house when she was three. And the photo of Iris and Jack. She should get a frame for it, she thought, display it downstairs on the mantel where Iris had only photographs of her alpacas and beautiful shots of the ranch, the pasture at dusk, a field at sunrise, the red barn in bright sunshine, a bird perched on the roof.

The moment the door had shut behind Dylan and Lindy, Colt had pulled her into his arms and she'd practically fallen against him, spent and sad. He'd just held her by the door for minutes. She'd told him she just wanted to go upstairs and lie down and try to let all she'd heard and all she'd wondered about settle. He'd put both his hands on her face and kissed her, then looked at her and told her he was there for her, even if it was three

in the morning, come on in and they'd talk about
it or not talk at all.

Oh, Colt, she thought now. *I wish you were in
this bed with me.*

*Not talking. Just behind me, your arms around
me tight, spooned.*

She looked at the time on her phone. 1:18 a.m.
She flopped over to her right side, wondering if
he was sleeping. Ryder had been quiet all night,
going to bed easily.

*What changed you irrevocably, Aunt Iris? That
you couldn't have children or that you gave up
the man you loved because you didn't believe
he'd be happy without children of his own?* She
was pretty sure it was the latter. Ava had known
since she was twenty-two that she wouldn't be
able to have kids and she had a feeling she and
her aunt had been dealing with the same medical condition. When she'd gotten the news from
her doctor, Ava had felt that something had been
taken away from her, a choice, but she hadn't assumed it would mean she'd be alone forever or
had to be. Seemed to Ava that Iris had decided
it did mean that for *her*, though, despite the op-
tions, such as adopting or becoming a stepmother.

Iris had turned inward, away from family, and
had isolated herself on the ranch, making it her

sanctuary, filling it with her beloved alpacas. But like Vivi and Maria had said, she'd been content.

Except now Ava didn't believe *that*. Iris had known she was getting sick, very sick, and she'd gone looking for that photo and tucked it in the pocket of her favorite cardigan. She'd loved that man and had given him up. Maybe there was more to it than his wanting a big family. Maybe there wasn't. Ava would never know. A choice had been presented to Iris in the form of a marriage proposal, three of them, and sworn declarations that her inability to have kids didn't matter to him, and Iris had said no. She'd made her choice, and Ava knew she had to respect that. Her great-aunt had had her reasons. End of story.

She felt tears welling and let herself have a good cry. Then she got up and went into the bathroom and splashed cool water on her face. But on the way back to her bedroom, she stopped and turned the other way. And headed to Colt's room.

At his door, she listened for signs he was awake but all was quiet. She slowly turned the knob and went inside. Colt was lying on his side, facing the bassinet, the moonlight just enough that she could see his eyes were closed. She tiptoed to the bed and slipped in under the covers, spooning herself against him, her eyes wide open on Ryder, who was sleeping.

Colt's arm wrapped around her and pulled her even closer, and tears welled in her eyes again, but she kept looking at sweet Ryder, his bow lips quirking, and all she could think was that Iris didn't have to say goodbye to her true love. Ava *did* believe that Jack would have been very happy to have his Iris, whether they adopted children or not. She could feel the depth of his love in every word Dylan and Lindy had said.

"He would have been happy with Iris," Ava whispered. "They could have adopted. Or not. But they would have had each other."

"Agreed," he said, kissing the side of her head.

"Why didn't she believe him?" she asked. "I believed him. But then again, I believed my fiancé when he told me it didn't matter, that we'd adopt. He was talking in the abstract then. He didn't really mean it but he didn't realize it. Until he was about to actually marry me."

Colt leaned his head against hers. "Except that guy wasn't your one true love, Ava."

She froze, and she could tell he felt her suddenly stop breathing because he did, too.

For a moment.

Please, Colt Dawson, don't say, He's out there and you'll find him.

Please, God, don't let him say that.

"No, Ava Guthrie, he was not your one true love," Colt repeated, wrapping his arm more tightly around her.

She breathed again, her eyes closing.

He didn't add, *I know because I am.*

But right then, in that moment, she believed he was thinking it.

The kisses started on her neck, up to her ear, then down to her shoulder, a finger slipping in to move her T-shirt out of the way of his lips. *Ah, never stop kissing me*, she thought.

She turned around so that she was facing him, and he kissed her so passionately her legs would have given out had she not been lying down. He kissed all over her face, her eyelids, her forehead, then her chin. Along her collarbone. She felt his hands lifting up her shirt and over her head and onto the floor it went. She did the same with his.

He was wearing those sexy sweatpants again, low slung, and she wriggled them down his hips. No boxer briefs this time. Just pure Colt Dawson.

He slipped his hand into the sides of her pj bottoms and inched them down, kissing her neck, her collarbone again, and then lower until he found her breasts, his hand and mouth busily exploring. She barely felt him take off her underwear as he kissed her stomach, her thighs, his lips and tongue making their way back to her belly button, then lower and lower until her legs parted and she almost screamed, jamming a fist in her mouth.

She opened her eyes and he was looking right at her, poised above her. His hands were on either side of her face as he kissed her, and then she could barely think at all as she felt him nudging inside her, deeper, harder. With his every groan and thrust she could barely keep herself from screaming his name, her nails in his shoulders.

I love you, Colt Dawson was the last thing she remembered thinking before a beautiful explosion of pleasure. And then suddenly she was back spooned against him, naked, satisfied, a dopey smile on her face that she couldn't imagine ever fading.

She was with her one true love.

The truth of Ava's story was that Colt was leaving the day after Christmas and taking his baby son with him. But she had the next week and a half with Colt, with the baby she adored, and she was going to make the most of it. She needed Colt in all ways right now and she'd let herself have this. How she'd let him go she had no idea.

If Iris had felt anything for Jack the way Ava felt for Colt, she could easily imagine how heartbroken Iris had been. Ava had always been looking for a deeper connection to the aunt she never had the opportunity to know. Now she had it.

It would take a Christmas miracle to change Ava's story, and even though she knew how the story ended, she'd still hope, still fantasize, still dream of three stockings on the mantel every year, hers, Colt's and baby Ryder's.

Chapter Fourteen

A week later, Christmas festival day, Colt unfolded the last of the forty chairs around the four long rented tables. The crafts area was set up across from the alpaca pasture for inspiration for young ornament makers. He glanced at the time on his phone. It was just before 7:00 a.m., and the festival would begin in one hour. Based on the number of emails and calls Ava had gotten—will there be bathroom access (two port-a-potties), do alpacas eat children's hair if they get too close to the fence (no), how many ornaments can each person make (one)—they were expecting *a lot* of people.

Ava came out of the house with the tablecloths, her blond hair shining in the sun. They couldn't have asked for nicer weather. It was forty-four degrees three days before Christmas—in Wyoming. A bright blue sky. She looked happy but a little nervous, a little stressed.

She had her elves, though—him, of course, and Dylan and Lindy, who'd also be in their of-

ficial festival-helper Prairie Hills Alpaca Ranch
sweatshirts, which Colt had ordered a bunch
of, and Vivi and Maria, who'd be arriving at
7:40 a.m. with the tons of Christmas cookies
they'd baked. Vivi had picked up her and Maria's sweatshirts a few days ago so that she could
add a little rhinestone pizzazz.

As Ava unfolded a tablecloth, they each took
an end, and Colt thought about last night—*every*
night the past week since their dinner with Dylan
and Lindy, when Ava had finally learned her
great-aunt Iris's story. Each night, they slept in
his bed, Colt taking care of the middle-of-the-
night wakings and feeding. Colt now knew the
difference between an *I'm hungry* cry and a *my
diaper is sopping wet, change me now* cry. He
easily got the baby back to sleep—75 percent of
the time, anyway—but he'd come to understand
the 25 percent was baby related, not because of
anything he was doing wrong. He'd finished reading his fatherhood book, knowing what to expect
in the months ahead, such as teething and solid
foods, and he was excited about those changes
and new milestones to come instead of his chest
tightening that he'd get it all wrong.

What he wasn't excited about: leaving in three
days. He'd tried to picture himself back at God-

frey and Dawson, in a suit, his Italian leather
shoes, his dad's briefcase, boarding a plane, driving, the hotels, the emptiness.

The lack of Ava in his life.

Not waking up with her. Not going to sleep
with her every night, curled against him. Not getting up at 5:00 a.m. to let the alpacas in the pasture, to set out their straw and change their water
and clean their pen.

Hanging up his cowboy hat—again.

You were never staying here, he reminded
himself. *This was a temporary stop. A place to
get the truth about Ryder. A place to breathe for a
few weeks. A good deal between you and a good
woman. You were never staying.*

"I can't believe festival day is here," Ava said.
"It felt like so long ago when I first decided to
hold it. And now it's here. Christmas just two
days away." She glanced up at him, squinting in
the bright sun. "Just two more full days with you
and Ryder," she added.

"Two more days," he repeated, his voice flat.

"How am I going to leave this place?" he asked.
The ranch had become a part of him. A piece of
him. The red barn. The white farmhouse. The
pastures. The alpacas.

"Don't," she said, her chin lifted, her voice firm. "Stay."

He stared at her, the tablecloth fluttering and going kind of sideways.

"There. I made it official—I'm asking. Stay, Colt. You and Ryder."

Words wouldn't come. He looked at her, and she was waiting for an answer. But she seemed to know he couldn't respond to that and grabbed the tablecloth, straightening it. She jogged over to the porch and stacked a few baskets of supplies and came back over with them, setting out three on each table, then ran back for the rest.

"Ava."

She frowned. "I know. You're going home. In two days. You never said otherwise. I was just hoping. Foolishly."

A pickup came up the drive—Dylan and Lindy, with Vivi's small silver car not far behind. He could see Maria in the passenger seat.

"My elves are here," she said, clearing her throat and heading over to the parking area he'd made, with a big sign indicating that, in a field just before the entrance to the ranch. A good hundred cars could fit comfortably in there with space to maneuver, and since people would be coming and going, that seemed about right. Plus, folks could always park along the side of the long drive up to the ranch.

Ava, he wanted to call. But what would he say? He wasn't staying. Even though he wanted to. He needed to go home, he needed to go back to work. His life was in Bear Ridge.

Even if his heart was here. That heart would get trampled eventually. Irrevocably.

He'd go home. He'd buy a ranch house. Maybe he'd finally get that horse. Not quite a working ranch, but at least he'd have the land, the Wyoming wilderness beyond. The horse. He'd visit the animal shelter and see about a dog.

He looked around, at the house, the barn, the pastures, the alpacas grazing in the half-melted snow. Leaving here would hurt.

So don't go, a voice inside him said. *Stay, like Ava said.*

But another voice was a firm Simon Cowell *no*. He didn't belong here. This wasn't home. The way he felt about Ava was complicated but it couldn't be love. He didn't believe in that anymore.

He'd come here for a reason. And now it was time to go.

His time with Ava had been special, almost otherworldly, and probably because it wasn't quite real, it wasn't permanent. It was never going to be.

Their relationship would change the way relationships did. It would get sour and ugly. She'd want this, he'd not want to give that, and they'd be in a cold war like his marriage.

He thought of the letter Jocelyn had written to Ava, the unfinished, awful letter.

Colt will never find out that Ryder isn't his child...

That numbness inched around his chest until it was replaced by something that felt hard and impenetrable.

He and Ava did have something special here. But it was time to go back to his life. To his responsibilities.

Colt heard a cry come from his monitor and went inside the house. Everything was about Ryder. Not Colt's love life. Not his sex life.

He'd left the baby in the kitchen in his swing while they took care of the tables, and now it was time to get Ryder in his stroller, which he could nap in easily while Colt served as security director for the event. He'd be keeping an eye on the pasture with the alpacas, making sure no one fed them—signs were posted not to—and that no one, like a rowdy group of teens—tried to do anything show-offy or dumb. If he needed someone to watch Ryder, he could always wheel the stroller

over to the refreshments table or find Dylan and
Lindy, which they'd prediscussed.

Everything was set. All they were waiting for
now was the clock to strike eight o'clock.

Colt went into the kitchen and got the jugs of
cider and the containers of eggnog, putting them
in a box he'd carry out. "I'll be back for you in
two secs," he told Ryder, who was happily batting
his giraffe rattle against the side of the swing,
giggling away.

He grabbed the box and brought it outside to
the refreshments table, which Vivi and Maria
were now sitting behind, covered tray upon tray
of Christmas cookies practically taking up the
whole table. He set out a few jugs of cider and
eggnog, and the sturdy cups.

"Hey, cowboy," Maria said, smiling at him,
rhinestones encircling the Prairie Hills Alpaca
Ranch logo imprinted in big letters on her red
sweatshirt. "You did some amazing work here."

"The ranch looks like a postcard," Vivi agreed,
looking around. "Absolutely beautiful and so festive. Thanks for helping our Ava."

Our Ava.

She was his Ava, too.

I made it official—I'm asking. Stay, Colt...

He saw her by the pasture, in her own red

ranch sweatshirt, which he'd had lined with thick fleece to keep them all warm, talking to the alpacas, probably filling them in on the big day. That there would be a lot of people staring at them and wanting to pet them.

How the hell he was going to walk away from this woman in two days, he had no idea.

He went back into the house and got Ryder changed and into his fleece, then put him in the stroller, his bag in the basket. There would be a lot for a baby to look at today.

Vehicles could be heard coming up the long driveway. Showtime. Colt glanced at his phone. A few minutes before eight o'clock.

With Ryder in his stroller, he took his position by the pasture, looking like a friendly dad in his red Prairie Hills Alpaca Ranch sweatshirt instead of the eagle-eyed guard he'd be today.

Streams of people started coming past the entrance to the ranch, pointing at the pasture, looking all around. He could see Dylan and Lindy directing. Ava was staying put on the other side of the alpaca pasture and already had a crowd around her, people asking questions and reaching to pet the big white alpacas, Lorelai and Rory. Star was off to the side by herself, as usual.

Lone wolf like me, he thought. *Just our way.*

Maybe one of these gals pissed you off and you decided you'd had it with alpacas, so you keep to yourself. That's me now. On my own. Me and Ryder.

Now he was talking to an alpaca? In his head. Great.

Ava had tried hard to put her very short, very unsatisfying conversation with Colt out of her head once people started arriving. Now the festival was in full swing—it really had been all morning through the early afternoon. Folks tended to stay about an hour, then left, a stream of new people coming to take their place. In just over an hour, the festival would end. And Ava could definitely call it a success.

Vivi and Maria had had to get their *third* round of trays of Christmas cookies from the kitchen, and the cider and eggnog needed replacing every hour. Colt had smartly suggested they order a banner for behind the refreshments table with the ranch logo, website and telephone number and that let folks know that come spring, there would be children's camps and workshops to register for, and she'd noticed people looking at it, some taking photos to have the info. Dylan had taken charge of the crafts table, and hundreds of ornaments were made, children laughing over the alpaca fleece puffing out on their handiwork, Maria coming over to help when Dylan looked like he might lose his mind. Lindy had become the day's photographer, taking hundreds of photos of people of all ages with the alpacas and handing them over. Colt had ordered a case of film for the instamatic camera, and no one had walked away without their photo. Ava must have given the same talk about alpacas, answered the same questions about two hundred times.

And she loved every minute of it.

Colt had set up Bluetooth speakers so that Christmas songs were playing low but still audible around the barn and pasture. From her spot just inside the alpaca pasture, treats in her pocket if she needed to lure one over to say hi to a group, she could see Colt on the gated side of the pen, watching the crowd like a hawk, his trusty sidekick deputy with his bear-ears fleece hoodie beside him in the stroller. So far, there'd been no trouble, no one trying to feed the alpacas a Christmas cookie or jumping the fence to try to ride one of them.

Ava stood in the bright sunshine, Pecan and Cookie beside her, telling a little girl that no, alpacas didn't eat hamburgers, her favorite food.

They were actually vegetarians. She could feel her great-aunt Iris with her—in fact, Ava felt her presence so strongly that a peace came over her. *We did it, Iris. You trusted me, and we did it. The ranch is back. Everything is going to be okay.*

But out of the corner of her eye, she saw Colt watching a group of older teenagers, boys and girls, giggling and pointing at the alpacas. One of the boys went up to the edge of the fence and called out, "Hey, ugly, over here!" Then he turned to take a selfie, laughing and shoving the phone in his sweatshirt pocket. But then he got a weird smile on his face—a troublemaker's smile—and reached into his jean's pockets.

Colt moved a few feet toward the group, staring them down until the boy pulled his hands out of his pockets and held them up as if to show he didn't have anything. The teens then headed toward the refreshments table. Then she saw Colt go back where he'd left the stroller, turning in circles, calling out, "Ryder. Ryder!"

What was this? She ran to that side of the pasture, looking for the stroller.

She didn't see it.

"Ryder's gone," he said, his voice barely audible. He began rushing around in every direction, searching the area. "His stroller is gone."

She ran out of the pasture, locking it behind her, and caught up with Colt, who was turning in circles, scanning wildly for the stroller.

The panic on his face scared the hell out of her.

Colt pulled out his phone. "I'm calling the police."

"Colt," she said, grabbing his arm. "There! He's right there. That woman with the long hair is pushing his stroller toward the house."

Colt stuffed his phone in his pocket and raced over, weaving his way through the crowds. She hurried after him.

But when he got up to the woman, who was still heading toward the porch steps, he stopped. And she could practically see all the air whoosh out of him.

"Haley!" he called.

Ava froze, her shoulders relaxing so hard she was surprised she didn't fall over. It was his sister who had Ryder.

Haley turned around, her hands firmly on the stroller. "I was looking all over for you! I just got here a little while ago, planning to surprise you, and saw Ryder's stroller totally unattended by the alpaca pasture so I figured I'd wheel him over by the house and sit with him until I spotted you."

Colt leaned his head back, letting out one hell

of an exhale. "I was just two feet away, watching a group of rowdy teens," he explained. "When I got back two seconds later and Ryder was gone—" He bent down, and she knew his panic hadn't abated. "Oh God. I thought someone took him."

"I'm so sorry, Colt," Haley said, tears welling in her eyes. "I should have just stayed in that spot with him. I'm so sorry."

He unbuckled Ryder from the stroller and held him against him, his hands protective on his back and bottom.

Haley looked at Ava. "I didn't mean to scare you both. I'm so sorry."

Ava put a hand on Haley's arm. "It's okay. Ryder was always safe with you, Haley. Colt just had a terrible scare."

"He's ready for his nap," Colt said through gritted teeth, "so I'll go put him down. Ava, you can ask Dylan to go on guard duty. Or Lindy. She's probably fiercer."

Ava bit her lip. "You okay?"

He didn't respond.

She and Haley looked at each other. Both of them worried.

Colt headed up the porch steps, leaving the stroller.

Haley turned to Ava. "I'll go talk to him. Don't

let this ruin the rest of your big day. Everything's okay now."

Ava could barely find her voice. She nodded and watched Haley carry the stroller into the house.

Oh, Colt, she thought. She'd never seen that look on his face. When he'd realized his baby was gone.

She was desperate to go talk to him, but someone was asking her questions, a family with children, and she could barely hear them, barely process. She took in a breath and forced a smile at the group. Haley was with him. She'd talk him down.

But everything was not going to be all right. By now, she knew Colt Dawson.

He was going to blame himself for letting someone—albeit his sister—walk away with his child.

He was going to blame himself hard.

Colt sat in the rocking chair in his room, Ryder fast asleep across his lap, his head in the crook of Colt's arm. Haley had moved the desk chair over by the window a few feet away.

"This is who I am, Haley. I'm our father. I'm Bertrand Dawson. Someone who puts the job first, the four-month-old baby second. How could I have turned my back for one second? At a crowded event."

"You were two feet away, Colt. And if I hadn't walked off with his stroller, you would have been back in one second and everything would have been fine."

"But everything wasn't fine. Ryder disappeared. Anyone could have taken him." He looked at the baby in his arms, his son, whom he'd let down today.

The fear that had gripped him when he realized the stroller was gone. His heart had pounded like he'd never experienced before.

Haley leaned forward. "Don't you remember when Mom took me to the supermarket when I was like two years old while you stayed home with Dad because he wanted to take you to his office, and she was taking forever to choose between linguini or spaghetti in the pasta aisle and when she went to put the box in the shopping cart, I was gone? Gone. Nowhere to be found up or down the aisle. She was sobbing. The manager had to call the police because no one could find me."

He did remember hearing about that. "But you were under a display area with those plastic flags. You were fine."

"So was Ryder. Mom was the best, Colt. If it happened to her, it can happen to anyone."

He looked down at Ryder. "Well, it will damned well never happen again."

"That's fine. But don't think it means that you're a neglectful father. You're anything but."

He leaned his head back, letting out a long exhale. He had to admit, she'd made him feel better about what happened.

"You've been here just about three weeks, Colt. Surely this place worked its ranch magic on you. Don't let this one incident derail all the good stuff."

"It has been good," he said, looking out the window.

"You and Ava seem close," she said so nonchalantly that he knew she wanted the details.

"We've helped each other out." He looked down at Ryder. "She wants me to stay. Me and Ryder."

Haley gasped. "So I was right. You two have gotten *very* close. I like Ava. I know her from the diner. She used to come in a couple times a week. Likes minestrone soup and pie, all kinds."

He didn't know she liked minestrone soup. There was actually a lot he didn't know about her because their time here was so busy, the days long but packed. "I'm going home the day after

tomorrow," he said. "Back to work. Ryder will go
to the excellent day care at the Dawson Family
Guest Ranch. Maisey's never had a kid go missing on her. Trust me, I asked when I first started
bringing him there."

"Or you could stay here, and Aunt Haley
would not mind one bit driving two hours to see
you and my nephew. In fact, I'd like to."

He raised an eyebrow. "Oh really."

"You deserve this, Colt. The ranch. Real love.
True love."

True love. Dylan and Lindy flashed into his
mind, their clasped hands and beaming faces,
their story about Iris and Jack. Colt did believe
in the power of *ranches*, of horses and cattle and
sheep and chickens and hay. He did not believe
in real love. True love.

His phone pinged with a text and he glanced
over at the little table beside the rocking chair.
Ava. Asking how he was doing.

I'm not fine, that much I know.

That was all he knew for sure.

Chapter Fifteen

For the past two days, since the festival, since Ryder had disappeared for a very stressful minute, Ava had hoped for a miracle, that Colt would do like Jack Howard had and get down on one knee in front of the alpacas and propose. She would say yes. The *first* time. But he'd been distant. Very much so. Exactly what she'd been afraid of.

The night of the festival, Haley had gone back to Bear Ridge that same day, though she'd originally hoped to stay over, telling Ava that she knew Ava and Colt needed some time alone and that she thought she was able to make Colt feel better. Vivi and Maria had been godsends, putting themselves on cleanup duty, Dylan and Lindy folding up the tables and chairs into the barn so they could be picked up by the rental company. With the exception of a one-minute period, the festival had been wonderful, everything Ava had hoped.

That one minute had seemed to reinforce something for Colt; something that he was likely rationalizing. He'd told her he was leaving, going back to Bear Ridge, before the incident even happened. She'd asked him to stay and he wasn't staying.

Now, on Christmas Eve morning, her chest ached just thinking about it. *I want you to stay. You and Ryder.* The words coming straight from her heart. Her most fervent Christmas wish.

Not going to come true.

Since that night, he'd put himself on overtime around the ranch, cleaning out the alpaca pen when that was her job, taking care of the returns of the rentals for the festival, surprising her with orders of quality hay and pellets that he'd never mentioned placing. She'd just find them stacked neatly in the barn. She wouldn't have to buy anything for a few months. He'd fixed what needed fixing. Did what needed doing. Lightbulbs were changed. Smoke detectors were tested.

The night of the festival, she'd knocked on his bedroom door about two hours after she knew he would have put Ryder to bed. She'd wanted to give him some space, some time to digest what had happened, to let whatever his sister had said get in there.

There was no response to her knock, and her heart had seized in her chest. She'd gone in anyway. He was either sleeping or pretending to. As if he'd have been able to sleep after what had happened. She knew him too well for that.

How she'd wanted to get into bed with him as they had for the past week.

You have to let him go, she'd told herself. *It's what he wants.*

So she'd turned back, gone to her own room. That was the way it would be from here on in, so she might as well get used to it.

She hadn't knocked last night. Instead, she stayed in her own room, finally finishing his Christmas present, the green alpaca-fleece scarf that actually came out much better than she imagined, and wondering how she'd get through a wedding in the morning, a ceremony in which she and Colt would be the only guests, the witnesses, the photographer and videographer.

Now, the happy couple stood by the alpaca pasture, cooing to the six gals, and Ava surprised herself by feeling…joyful. She was happy for them, this beautiful, sweet couple who'd given her more than they could ever know. The story she needed. And their happiness, their belief in love and marriage, made her feel hopeful about the world. They were faith in itself.

Plus, they'd been gifted with another perfect-weather day for another special event. It was cold, but bearable in the thirties, the sunshine helping. The minister was due any minute, so Ava had been using the last half hour since the couple had arrived to take photos with Lindy's cell phone, which she'd said had an excellent camera.

She stood to the side of the bride and groom, snapping away on her phone, while Colt was videographer with Dylan's video camera. He'd been subdued this morning, though he'd been warm enough to the couple, shaking their hands, wishing them well. Yesterday, after a day of Colt keeping to himself and going about his work on the ranch so quietly she sometimes didn't realize he was in the barn at the same time she was, he'd surprised her again when a delivery truck pulled up with a trellis and a red carpet runner for the ceremony. She'd gasped at the thoughtfulness. He'd had it positioned right in front of the alpaca pasture, the barn just to the left, and then spent a half hour entwining white lights around it.

That was Colt Dawson. Kind. Got stuff done. Went above and beyond.

When Dylan and Lindy had arrived this morning, they'd looked at the trellis and hugged each other, then hugged Ava and Colt, so thankful, so happy. Lindy wore her beautiful white tea-length satin dress, a lovely bouquet of pink and white roses in her hand. Dylan wore a suit and shiny black shoes, and they were such the picture of hope and love and all good things that Ava almost burst into tears.

The minister arrived and then soon enough, the wedding was underway.

Ava teared up as they vowed to love, honor and cherish each other till death did them part. And they'd written vows of their own. To believe in each other, no matter what.

Ava glanced at Colt, but his face was partially hidden by the video camera. He had to be touched by all this. All this…love. Belief. Belief in each other.

And then it was over, the marriage license signed, hugs, a toast with mimosas, light on the champagne since Dylan was driving them back to town. They were secretly married.

Colt gave Dylan back his video camera, Ava gave Lindy back her phone, and she'd made sure to get a few shots of her own.

"I feel like Iris and Jack were both watching the ceremony," Dylan said, an arm around his brand-new wife. "I think they were both really happy for us."

Ava's chest squeezed. "I think so, too."

There were more hugs, promises to send Ava photos, and then they were in their car. "Merry Christmas," they both called in unison as they drove off.

"Merry Christmas," Ava called back, waving at the car until it disappeared through the gate of the ranch. She sighed wistfully. "That was really beautiful. And I think Dylan is right. I think Iris and Jack were watching and that it gave them back something."

He squeezed her hand and nodded and for a moment they just watched the alpacas, moving about the pasture, Star off to the side, eyeing them. She walked toward them, sticking her long neck over the fence.

Colt walked over and patted her side. "Hey, Star. Merry Christmas."

The alpaca lifted her head and walked back over to her favorite spot, then lay down in the sunshine.

Colt laughed, a sound she'd missed for the past two days. "I have something for you," he said. "A Christmas present, I mean. Just a little something."

Her heart lifted. "I have something for you, too. And same, just a little something."

He put his arm around her, and for a moment it was like old times. Old times that had lasted two and a half weeks.

What she would give for their times to last forever.

"Hey look," she said, pointing out the window of the living room where a light snow had begun to fall. "White Christmas."

"Dylan and Lindy are lucky it held off till after the wedding," he said. "Though those two probably wouldn't have cared if it had been pouring rain."

She smiled. "True."

When they'd gotten back inside, they'd gone to their rooms and brought their presents down and put them under the tree, where there were several brightly wrapped gifts for Ryder, ones they'd ordered over the past couple of weeks. Ava had gotten the baby a pair of adorable pajamas and a pair of fleece booties with little alpacas on them.

They stood in front of the tree, so festive, and each picked up the gift with their name on the tag, then sat on the sofa.

"You first," she said.

He shook the wrapped box and smiled. "I have no idea what this could be."

"Open it." She really hoped he'd like it. And that he'd wear it. But maybe when he got back home, it would go on top of his closet shelf with his cowboy hat, where all reminders of the ranch would stay.

He ripped off the wrapping paper and opened the box, taking out the scarf, the Prairie Hills Alpaca Ranch label sewn in. He grinned and wrapped it around his neck. "You made this," he said, looking at her. "Very, very impressive. And it's so soft. Thank you, Ava. I love it."

I wished you loved me, she thought.

"Now you," he said.

She picked up the wrapped gift from her lap. It wasn't heavy but it wasn't light. She ripped off the paper and opened the box, wondering what it could be.

She moved the white tissue paper, her hand flying to her heart. It was a picture frame, mother of pearl. But not just any picture frame. There was a hand-painted alpaca along the left side. It was Star. *Their* Star. The loner. Right down to her silver-gray eyes and the clump of hair on her cinnamon-colored head that was slightly lopsided. Along the bottom of the frame, script read: *True love.*

"It's for the photograph of Iris and Jack," he said. "I had it special made from a website I found."

She had to try really hard not to cry.

Oh, Colt, she thought. For a man who didn't think he was a romantic… "It's beyond," she managed to say. "I love it so much. Thank you."

She put it on the coffee table and turned to give him an awkward, distant hug but she got the real thing instead. He drew her to him, enfolding her in his arms, his head leaning against hers.

"Merry Christmas, Ava," he whispered.

"Merry Christmas, Colt," she whispered back.

Her laptop, on the far side of the coffee table, dinged. Great timing, email.

He sat up, moving slightly away, their knees no longer touching.

Don't make this any more awkward or painful, she told herself, forcing her gaze on the laptop, which she slid over. "I must have gotten three hundred emails since the festival. People really enjoyed it. We definitely achieved what we set out to."

He nodded. "The ranch is exactly where it needs to be. It helps me feel better about leaving knowing that. You're set here, Ava. Just keep doing what you're doing."

Set. Hardly. How could she be set without him? Without Ryder?

She didn't have just one true love. She had two. Big and little.

So ask. Bring it up. Don't walk on eggshells like you've been doing the past two days.

She sucked in a breath. "I guess that answers that question. You're leaving as planned." She could barely look at him. She'd barely been able to get the words out.

"It was always the plan," he said—gently. "I need to go home. I need to get back to work. I was always leaving Christmas morning."

She looked at him. "I was hoping being here would change you. Irrevocably," she added on a ragged whisper. "In a good way."

He reached for her hand, his gaze soft on hers. But he didn't say anything.

She felt tears pricking her eyes and stood, taking her frame and the box and the wrapping paper, willing herself not to cry in front of him. "Well, good night, then," she said. "Merry Christmas."

He waited a beat, and she was so damned hopeful. But all he said was, "Merry Christmas, Ava."

Some of her Christmas wishes had come true. But the one she'd been hoping for with all her heart? Not that one.

Colt lay in bed, his head on the soft alpaca-fleece-filled pillow, the duvet that he couldn't imagine ever sleeping without up over his shoulders. It was just after midnight. Ryder's head was turned to face him, his lips giving that quirk that Colt loved so much, and in that moment, all moments like that, where it was just him and his son and the tiniest details about Ryder, Colt felt okay, that all was right with his world, that everything made sense.

Ryder started crying out of nowhere, and Colt waited a few seconds. But it was crying like last week, when it took an hour to calm him down. He wanted to pick him up and go into Ava's room, not because he didn't think he could handle it, but because he knew he could. And he just wanted to be with her, at just after midnight. Which meant it was Christmas.

You're not making any sense, he thought, taking Ryder over to the changing pad and making quick work of his diaper.

I was hoping being here would change you. Irrevocably. In a good way.

It had, he knew. He'd become a better father, even if he'd made a terrible mistake at the festival. He wouldn't forgive himself so fast for that, his mother, who could have won Mother of the Year awards every year, notwithstanding.

He would go home just hours from now, back to the house he never wanted to live in, back to the company he'd never wanted to work for.

Like he'd just thought, he wasn't making any sense. Nothing made sense without Ava Guthrie. But that was part of the reason he was leaving.

He would have beautiful memories of their time together, the restoration that had gone on inside him. Christmas. The gift she'd given him of time with his child, time on the ranch. Time with her.

When he left, when he was back home, thinking about Ava months from now, years from now, nothing would sully the memories. No bitterness as they fought over this or that. No ugliness as they lied to each other about the littlest thing.

The biggest things.

He and Ava, their experience here at the Prairie Hills Alpaca Ranch, would always be as magical as this Christmas was.

That was the only thing that made sense to him right now.

* * *

Colt had slept like hell. Ryder almost slept through the night, waking just that once. After changing him, Colt had given him a bottle, and then gotten him back to sleep by singing "Silent Night," clearly his favorite Christmas song.

As he'd passed Ava's room on the way up the stairs about twelve thirty in the morning, he'd almost tapped on her door. But he'd kept going, his chest seizing. He hadn't been able to get to sleep, so he'd packed his and Ryder's stuff, in the same duffels he'd come with.

Now, he glanced out the window, at the gently falling snow. He got out of bed and stared down at the empty alpaca pasture, thinking of them on their straw in the barn. He'd miss them. He'd miss this place.

He'd miss Ava.

Ryder was stirring, and Colt picked him up and got him changed and dressed in his striped red-and-green fleece pj's, a Christmas gift from his aunt Haley. Colt set the bags by the door, then wrapped his hand-knit scarf around his neck, which just very faintly smelled of Ava's perfume.

He left the bags and took Ryder downstairs to give him his bottle, surprised to find Ava in the kitchen, sitting at the table with coffee, another mug waiting by the carafe.

"Merry Christmas," she said so brightly that he knew she was hurting.

"I don't know how I'm going to just walk out the door," he said.

She stood up, her hazel eyes on his. "So don't. Stay."

"I can't." He turned to settle Ryder in his swing and then made up his bottle.

"You're just going to give us up? Like Iris did Jack? That's it?"

Stab to the heart. He took Ryder from the swing and settled him on his lap, his head in the crook of his arm. "We always knew I was going back."

He fed Ryder, patting him gently on the back until he got that great big burp. Ava didn't even crack a smile.

"Will you hold him so I can get our bags from upstairs?" he asked.

She took the baby, cuddling him against her, her head leaning against Ryder's.

His heart so heavy, he trudged upstairs and got their bags, looking around the room for the last time.

Downstairs, she was still cuddling Ryder, telling him Merry Christmas.

"There are two wrapped gifts with his name under the tree. You can just put them in his bag. The ones you got him, too."

He brought the duffels into the living room, reaching under the tree and packing the gifts that he'd open at home.

Home.

He shook his head, everything feeling wrong.

He put the bags by the door and got on his coat and his cowboy hat, his green scarf around his neck. "Thank you for everything, Ava Guthrie."

She kissed Ryder's head and kneeled down to settle him in the car seat by the door, buckling him in. "I won't say goodbye, Ryder. I can't." She stood up and stared at Colt hard. "Tell me you don't love me and I'll let this go. I'll let you go."

Love. The word echoed in his head. It wasn't about love. It was about…self-preservation.

"Ava, I——" he began but there were no words.

She waited a few seconds, her shoulders slumping. "Just go," she said. "I can't take it. You don't love me and that's all there is to it."

"That's not all there is to it. Not by a long shot."

"Go," she said again, turning away.

He slid the duffels over each shoulder, and with the baby carrier in his hand, he walked out the door, his heart so heavy he was surprised he could walk.

He looked back toward the house, hoping to get a glimpse of Ava in the window, but she wasn't there.

He stopped in the barn, the alpacas looking up as he entered. "Merry Christmas," he said to them, surprised to see Star wasn't in her usual spot. She wasn't as close as the others were, but she was sitting nearer to them than he'd ever seen while he'd been at the ranch. "Maybe that's a little of Iris and Jack's magic," he said to Ryder. "I'd like to think it is."

He held up Ryder's car seat above the pen so that Ryder could see the alpacas one last time.

One last time. His chest ached with that thought.

Tell me you don't love me and I'll let you go...

He squeezed his eyes shut, then opened them, keeping his gaze firmly on his son. On his future. It was him and Ryder now. That was the way it was supposed to be from here on in.

A few minutes later, he was driving through the gates, the Prairie Hills Alpaca Ranch sign almost doing him in.

Chapter Sixteen

The day after Christmas, Colt was back at Godfrey and Dawson, the company on a skeleton staff since he and Brandon had agreed to give most of the staff the week between Christmas Eve and New Year's off. He'd barely caught up in the nine hours he'd been here, unable to think of anything but Ava.

Tell me you don't love me and I'll let you go...

Her anguished words had echoed in his head on the long drive home. All night long. This morning in the shower. On the way back here, to Godless and Dawdling.

He did love her.

He loved her so much he was going crazy with it.

What am I doing here? he asked himself, shaking his head.

He sat at his big cherry desk, staring at the time on his computer—five thirty—staring at his long list of emails, staring at his overflowing inbox of reports. He looked around the big corner office that had once been his grandfather's. That had once been his father's.

He didn't want to be here. In this chair. In this office. He swiveled toward the window and stared out, downtown Bear Ridge his view, the bustling small town full of people off the day after Christmas, taking advantage of sales, the shops still festive with lights and garland.

On his lunch hour, he'd gone to the bank where Jocelyn had her safe-deposit box. Haley met him there, just in case there were photos with the documents from the fertility clinic. If those were the documents in that box. He'd held his breath before turning the key the bank employee had given him.

But there was just a letter in there. This one finished. To him, from Jocelyn.

Dear Colt,
If you're reading this, I must be gone. I don't know how or why or what, so I'll just leave you this. I want you to know that I really did love you, despite...everything. I'm sorry for anything I did that might have upset you. In the end, just know I was very happy and I hope you will be, too. No matter what.
Jocelyn.

She was Jocelyn to the very end, leaving a "just in case" letter, a cryptic one, not admitting to anything but in case he had found out the truth, she was apologizing in her own way. He'd felt something give inside him, loosen. A bitterness dissipating.

He and Haley talked that over at lunch at the diner. "Thank God," Haley had said. "I was worried about you for a while there. Okay, until just now. And even Jocelyn hopes you'll be happy, Colt. So go back to the alpaca ranch and be happy."

He missed Ava so much it hurt. He missed the ranch, the barn, the alpacas. He thought of Ryder at the day care, dropped off bright and early this morning, and he knew he was well cared for there, but he wanted his son with him. Always.

He swiveled back around in his office chair just as Brandon Godfrey rapped on his office door. Brandon was a few years older, thirty-seven, with dark hair and dark eyes, his suit impeccable even at the end of the workday. He wore silver round glasses, his trademark. He'd had that same pair as long as Brandon had known him. A long time.

"I'm headed out," Brandon said. "Good to have you back."

"Tell me something, Brandon," Colt said. "Do

you ever think about leaving—I mean leaving the company?"

Brandon gaped. "Leave? Godfrey and Dawson? Lord, no. I live for this place. You know that."

"Think your son will follow in your footsteps?" he asked. Now that he thought about it, Brandon never brought his son around the office.

"Definitely not. Eli is fifteen and has big dreams to join the army and become a paratrooper medic. My shop talk bores him to death."

Huh.

"But what about the next Godfrey?" Colt asked.

Brandon shrugged. "You and I are the only Godfrey and Dawson here and there's hardly anything family-focused about a corporation, particularly our business of buying and selling businesses. It's about deals, not who runs the place. The sales director is a real up-and-comer—I've got my eye on him for VP. Smart moves, good employees will keep this place going. I don't think it has to be a Godfrey and a Dawson for the end of time. Though it's nice for the boardroom oil paintings."

Brandon and Colt had their photographs hanging in the boardroom. Huge ones, the same size as the oil paintings, but they'd hardly kept up that tradition.

"Brandon, if I left the company, I wouldn't be

leaving you in any kind of lurch? I'm thinking of moving to an alpaca ranch about two hours from here out in Prairie Hills." He thought of the stables he'd build. A few horses. Maybe some sheep, which were easy to add to an alpaca farm. And a dog, but he'd have to talk to Ava about that.

Brandon stared at him. "An alpaca ranch. Huh. Are they the same as llamas?"

Colt laughed. "No. Close, though."

"Well, you go move to that ranch. Raise that cute baby of yours out there. I'll miss you, but I'll take care of this place. You know that."

He did know that. "I won't be here in the morning, then."

Brandon walked around the side of the desk, and Colt stood and they embraced. "You take good care."

"You, too, Brandon."

Colt felt the weight of Wyoming lift off his shoulders. He pulled out his phone and texted Haley.

I just told Brandon I won't be here in the morning. Ever again.

She texted back: Dad would be proud of you.

For not keeping my promise?

For lasting as long as you did, Colt. You made him happy when it was important to do so. Now you need to make yourself happy.

He'd never thought of it that way, but it filled that ragged hole in his chest, the one that had burned for the past fourteen years.

He was going home. To an alpaca farm in Prairie Hills.

If the woman of the ranch would have him.

Two days after Christmas, Ava sat at the kitchen table with Maria and Vivi, each of them with their knitting projects. They'd decided to meet twice a week for an hour, and their time was coming to a close today. Ava looked at the cowl she was making and frowned at it; she was using round needles for the first time and it was taking her a while to get used to the flexible needles. She could use an extra hour of the experts' tips and tricks. Vivi was making a gorgeous argyle sweater and had the body done. Maria was working on multicolored socks for her sister's birthday.

Maria looked at the clock on the wall and put her knitting in her tote bag, then finished the rest of her coffee. She leaned forward to take a Christmas cookie from the plate in the center of the table. "How I can still bear to eat these is beyond me. I've had a hundred since the festival."

"Me, too," Vivi said, putting her knitting away, too, and then grabbing a snowman cookie. "Yum."

Ava laughed and took a reindeer, dunking it into her coffee. "I had a great time today. Thank you for inviting me into your knitting circle. I could use a few more hours of your expertise, though. My cowl is curling in on itself."

"Those do that," Vivi said. "It's not you."

"Yeah," Maria put in. "You're doing great."

Except for the crying. She'd burst into tears five minutes into her friends' arrival, filling them in on everything that had happened.

Now tears brimmed again.

"Maybe I'm too much like Iris now," she said, putting aside the frustrating cowl. "Alone at the ranch, spending my days talking to alpacas. She knew it was over for her and now I do, too." Tears brimmed again. She'd never feel about anyone the way she felt about Colt Dawson.

Vivi shook her head. "Iris closed herself off from love. You're not doing that."

Ava wrapped her hands around her coffee. "But Colt's gone."

"Oh, trust me," Maria said. "That man will be back. Mark my words."

"With the baby," Vivi said.

"To stay for good," Maria added.

She knew they were just being kind. But it was past Christmas now and there were no more miracles to be had.

"Oh gosh," Maria said, popping up. "I need to get home. I'm babysitting tonight."

Vivi got up, too. "We'll see you Thursday, same time. Feel free to eat all those cookies. They're good for a sore heart."

They both gave her warm hugs, then they were gone.

Ava put on her jacket and hat and went into the barn, sitting down in the alpaca pen on her own plot of straw.

Star came over and sat a few feet away, getting a pat. Pecan and Cookie eyed her, then resumed just staring into space. Lorelai and Rory were sitting in kush position in their favorite area, and Princess was standing in her section, staring at Ava with what really looked like compassion.

Sorry you're hurting, Princess's big brown eyes seemed to say.

Ava leaned back against the pen, wondering what Colt was doing, if he was still at the office. Or if he was now operating on Ryder's schedule and had him home from the day care at his cousin's ranch.

She heard a car coming up the drive and stood. Vivi and Maria must have forgotten something. She headed out, barely feeling the cold air on her face.

Because it wasn't a little red car pulling up beside the barn.

It was Colt Dawson getting out of a silver pickup she'd never seen before, his green alpaca-knit scarf wrapped around his neck, cowboy hat on his head.

Ava stood in front of the barn, and it was all he could do not to rush up to her and grab her into a hug. But he had Ryder's car seat in his left hand and he'd left on terms that still had him twisted in knots.

He walked up to her. "You asked me to tell you that I don't love you. And the reason I couldn't answer, couldn't say anything, is because it's not true. I do love you, Ava. So much."

Her eyes widened. "Let's go talk in the house before we all freeze."

He followed her up the porch steps into the warm hallway. He set Ryder's car seat on the floor, the baby's eyes still closed.

"I do love you, Ava," he said the moment the door closed. "I didn't want to admit it to myself because of everything that happened, but you made me believe again. Not just in love, but myself, what I want for myself and for Ryder. And that includes you. I love you and want to spend my life here with you."

She finally smiled then, relief flooding him. "Alpacas are pretty great, aren't they?"

He put his arms around her, reveling in the feel of her so close, her head against his chest. "What would you think about expanding the ranch?" he asked. "Horses, maybe some sheep, a very alpaca-friendly dog? I traded in the SUV for a cowboy's pickup," he added, gesturing out the window.

She grinned. "We do make a good team," she said, looking up at him.

"We do."

"I love you, too, Colt. So much. You and Ryder both."

He lifted her up in his arms and kissed her. "How about a Christmas Eve wedding of our own next year?"

She smiled and kissed him back. "Ryder can toddle down the aisle as your best man. All my Christmas wishes came true, after all."

He put his hands on either side of her beautiful face and kissed her. "And now we've got next Christmas covered, too."

He kneeled down to unbuckle Ryder, who didn't stir as Colt picked him up. Another Christmas miracle.

And then he and Ava headed upstairs to start the rest of their lives together—as a family.

* * * * *

*For more great single parent
holiday romances, try these stories:*

The Father of Her Sons
By Christine Rimmer

The Cowboy's Christmas Retreat
By Catherine Mann

Merry Christmas, Baby!
By Teri Wilson

*Available now wherever
Harlequin Special Edition books and
ebooks are sold!*

#2875 DREAMING OF A CHRISTMAS COWBOY
Montana Mavericks: The Real Cowboys of Bronco Heights
by Brenda Harlen
In the Christmas play she wrote and will soon star in, Susanna Henry gets the guy. In real life, however, all-grown-up Susanna is no closer to hooking up with rancher Dean Abernathy than she was at seventeen. Until a sudden snowstorm strands them together overnight in a deserted theater...

#2876 SLEIGH RIDE WITH THE RANCHER
Men of the West • by Stella Bagwell
Sophia Vandale can't deny her attraction to rancher Colt Crawford, but when it comes to men, trusting her own judgment has only led to heartbreak. Maybe with a little Christmas magic she'll learn to trust her heart instead?

#2877 MERRY CHRISTMAS, BABY
Lovestruck, Vermont • by Teri Wilson
Every day is Christmas for holiday movie producer Candy Cane. But when she becomes guardian of her infant cousin, she's determined to rediscover the real thing. When she ends up snowed in with the local grinch, however, it might take a Christmas miracle to make the season merry...

#2878 THEIR TEXAS CHRISTMAS GIFT
Lockharts Lost & Found • by Cathy Gillen Thacker
Widow Faith Lockhart Hewitt is getting the ultimate Christmas gift in adopting an infant boy. But when the baby's father, navy SEAL lieutenant Zach Callahan, shows up, a marriage of convenience gives Faith a son and a husband! But she's already lost one husband and her second is about to be deployed. Can raising their son show them love is the only thing that matters?

#2879 CHRISTMAS AT THE CHÂTEAU
Bainbridge House • by Rochelle Alers
Viola Williamson's lifelong dream to run her own kitchen becomes a reality when she accepts the responsibility of executive chef at her family's hotel and wedding venue. What she doesn't anticipate is her attraction to the reclusive caretaker whose lineage is inexorably linked with the property known as Bainbridge House.

#2880 MOONLIGHT, MENORAHS AND MISTLETOE
Holliday, Oregon • by Wendy Warren
As a new landlord, Dr. Gideon Bowen is more irritating than ingratiating. Eden Berman should probably consider moving. But in the spirit of the holidays, Eden offers her friendship instead. As their relationship ignites, it's clear that Gideon is more mensch than menace. With each night of Hanukkah burning brighter, can Eden light his way to love?

"You're cold," Dean realized, when Susanna drew her
knees up to her chest and wrapped her arms around her
legs, no doubt trying to conserve her own body heat as
she huddled under the blanket draped over her shoulders
like a cape.

"A little," she admitted.

"Come here," he said, patting the space on the floor
beside him.

She hesitated for about half a second before scooting
over, obviously accepting that sharing body heat was the
logical thing to do.

But as she snuggled against him, her head against
his shoulder, her curvy body aligned with his, there was
suddenly more heat coursing through his veins than Dean

had anticipated. And maybe it was the normal reaction for a man in close proximity to an attractive woman, but this was *Susanna*.

He wasn't supposed to be thinking of Susanna as an attractive woman—or a woman at all.

She was a friend.

Almost like a sister.

But she's not your sister, a voice in the back of his head reminded him. *So there's absolutely no reason you can't kiss her.*

Don't do it, the rational side of his brain pleaded. *Kissing Susanna will change everything.*

Change is good. Necessary, even.

When Susanna tipped her head back to look at him, obviously waiting for a response to something she'd said, all he could think about was the fact that her lips were *right there*. That barely a few scant inches separated his mouth from hers.

He only needed to dip his head and he could taste those sweetly curved lips that had tempted him for so long, despite all of his best efforts to pretend it wasn't true.

Not that he had any intention of breaching that distance.

Of course not.

Because this was *Susanna*.

No way would he ever—

Apparently the signals from his brain didn't make it to his mouth, because it was already brushing over hers.

Don't miss
Dreaming of a Christmas Cowboy *by Brenda Harlen,
available December 2021 wherever
Harlequin Special Edition books and ebooks are sold.*

Harlequin.com

HSEEXP1121

Get 4 FREE REWARDS!

We'll send you 2 FREE Books plus 2 FREE Mystery Gifts.

Harlequin Special Edition books relate to finding comfort and strength in the support of loved ones and enjoying the journey no matter what life throws your way.

FREE Value Over **$20**